Something in the Water

By
Brian Matta

Lost Pilot Press

ISBN: 978-1-7353275-7-0
Copyright 2024
Book Design by Brian Matta
Lost Pilot Press

Content

As You Burst at the Seams

It was August 24th when Neil Grivers popped like a grape while driving home from church. His wife in the passage seat at the time screamed as what felt like homemade jelly splashed all over her new dress. At least that's what she told the police. Covered head to toe in a bright red juice. Her piercing blue eyes were the only thing keeping their attention from the horror. She muttered that he kept repeating a fact from a news headline over and over again.

When they arrived on the scene, they didn't believe the report. What remained was all gelatinous. There shouldn't have been that much blood. Stating the inside of the car was covered in a red film. There were no entrails or appendages of recognizable note. Merely blackened bits no one could decipher what part of the body they were from.

The first question I asked was how could this happen. However, by the end of the week there were four more cases just like this one. A person was repeating a fact faster and faster until they burst. Like an Obsessive Compulsive that keeps walking through the same door. Caught in a loop. But that didn't make any sense. Even if it's a phenomenon how could it be reaching this many people.

The investigation was a doozey. I spoke to the investigating office about the Grivers case, but he told me to scram. Even after I told him I wasn't the press just a private citizen interested in the case. Other people from the group chat had the same problem with law enforcement in their areas too.

The evidence compiled from all these cases around the country was not adding up. The people who exploded were different races, genders, ages, and so on. It wasn't spontaneous combustion because they didn't become a pile of ash. They exploded like they were bags of blood.

Some in the chat suggested that they were targeted by the CIA or another one of the surveillance agencies. This theory was due to the fact that two or three of the exploded were disgruntled former employees of the federal government. However, there were multiple holes in that theory. The rest of these explosions couldn't be disinformation agents and why does the CIA want to explode these people.

When this question was brought up in the thread there was a pause, a silence if you will because it shed light another unan-swered question, why did we care about these people? At this point we weren't able to answer that. Maybe we just became obsessed.

We were so obsessed that a few of us began to meet in person. Two or three at the beginning, but after about a month there were six core members who would meet and talk. We lived in the same vicinity, so we would take turns sleeping on each other floors. It was fun. Most of us had podcasts or websites dedicated to all sorts of conspiracy theories. We'd be on each other's shows and plan events. So we had plenty of material to talk about.

These exploding bodies were still happening, but they became background noise. We'd collected the news articles and filed them away and updated our data. Maybe recap the cases on a podcast or in an article, but that was about it. We were so busy that it mostly became forgotten. Until a viewer commented that they wanted to hear a full update of our findings.

We decided that was a great idea. We could all come together and write it as a collaborative effort. Some of us were even saying that we might have enough evidence to make a book out of it all. We scheduled a meeting on Memorial Day weekend, so we'd have three days to write and research, finally bang it all out. It was my turn to host, so I cleaned my apartment, went grocery shopping, made sure my printer had ink, and bought a classroom sized dry erase board. We were going all out on this one.

I also found these cheap mattresses to lay out on my living room floor and hallway. The last time it was my turn everyone complained how my apartment wasn't suitable for guests. I offered them a hardwood floor for their sleeping bags. Everyday in the group chat they were making fun of me. They shut up real quick once they saw what I had done.

After the initial rubbing by everyone we began to set up our excursion to the bottom to this bottomless pit. We hit a deadlock right away because there was a split in the six of us right down the middle. Three of us thought it was natural phenomenon like spontaneous human combustion while the other three thought it had something to do with the deep state. We all knew that this was a deep ravine, but chose to ignore it. However, when the chips were on the table we dug into our trenches and would not surrender.

It stopped the writing and fun time. Jim and Matt started to yell at each other. My neighbors were banging against the walls as I stepped in to break it up. Please keep your voices down. Apologizing, but it didn't stop the fury of those two. It was three hours before we decided this back and forth was not going anywhere. Matt would produce evidence of combustion and Jim would negate it and show the same evidence with it all pointing to the deep state. A vote was taken to table it until tomorrow. Jim was fine with it, but Matt seemed really hurt by the whole experience. Matt was quiet after that fight with Jim. So much so I thought he'd leave. The rest of the night he was mostly surfing on his laptop sipping his beer. Jim didn't seem that phased. He rejoined us as if nothing happened.

We decided to call it a night around 2:30 in the morning. We all dispersed and crashed onto our beds exhausted. I woke up out of my sleep with a jerk. My cat jumped on me meowing. I try to wave it away, but no luck. Jesus, fine. I got up in near pitch blackness. Stumbling not from the beers, but it was probably around 4am. I walked out of my room and noticed the kitchen light was on. Watched my cat go towards the light of the kitchen.

I followed and I heard someone talking. Christ these people were hardcore about research. The talking was low like someone being polite about watching a video. I walked in and saw it's Matt sitting at my kitchen table. His laptop was open, but he wasn't looking at. He was looking straight ahead. Muttering something. I walked up and asked if he's alright, but he just kept muttering. I couldn't make out what he's saying. All I knew was it was getting louder. His body burst like a ripe grape. The blast blew me back into the kitchen counter. It broke the glasses in the sink and knocked the table across the room splintering it into chunks. I thought it had burst my eardrums being so loud, but I'm not a doctor.

I tried to lift myself up, but Matt's syrupy remains were making me slip back onto the floor. He coated the kitchen and ceiling in a dripping red film. The rest of them most have been aroused by the shotgun blast that was Matt. Looking at the horror in silence finding me covered in viscera.

They asked me what happened. All I knew was he was muttering to himself and exploded. Like all the cases we'd been looking through. Do we call the police? I asked. We should. Because whatever did this killed our friend.

The police came and went. They took a sample of what was left of Matt. Took our stories. We were so hopeful to solve this whatever it was, but now we seemed more confused than ever. Everything we thought we knew crumbed. There was no smoking gun. It was all random. We found Matt's computer and he had hundreds of tabs open. It didn't seem possible how could the computer still work and not freeze.

We informed Matt's wife he was dead. She didn't take it well. No one did. After the funeral of what was left of Matt the five of us couldn't go on. There wasn't even a point. We were too shaken by what had happened. One or two were so freaked out that they thought we got too close to something. While the rest just didn't think it was right to continue. People wanted us to go on. To avenge Matt, but the road went another way.

We all just went back to our homes and did our own thing. Writing blogs or podcasting. Each other thought of having one another on again like before. But the pain got in the way. So we just put contacting each other on hold until this routine became everyday life. We didn't forget about each other more like we squeezed ourselves out of each other's lives.

I was trying to take a nap when out of the blue my phone started buzzing. I looked to see who it was and almost didn't recognize the name. Jim, who the fuck was Jim. Oh shit. I answered it. What's up. Jim said he wanted to meet me. I asked what for. He said he found something interesting about that case of exploding people. I was hazy on what he meant, but I said ok anyway. Driving to meet Jim I kept thinking of Matt before he exploded. Whatever he was muttering it seemed like he was forced. That image of his face played on a loop until I reached Jim's front door. I rang the bell and his wife answered. Polite plump woman who told me to take off my shoes. After offering me a cup of coffee Jim emerged from his basement.

He ignored his wife and waved me to join him down in the basement. As we descended the creaky steps, he hit me with all the evidence he had compiled over the months since Matt died. He opened the door at the bottom of his stairs and the walls were papered with pins and lines pointing to each other like in a clique movie we'd forgotten about.

He said he figured out the connection between all the people who had been exploding. It wasn't the CIA or some natural phenomenon, but genetic. I was stunned. How? He went on to say that he was going down a deep rabbit hole of CIA and intelligence which led only to a frustrating nowhere. He was lost and angry when he was thinking of this conversation with Matt. They were talking about their youth. They both had similar backgrounds. Both were inside cats and learned the internet alone in their rooms. However, Matt said that he had a heart murmur as a kid. He said it was genetic and most of his teenage years were spent trying to fix it. After this epiphany, he went back through his research and discover Greivers had a rare skin condition that made his skin flakey. Not only him, but every other member of the exploding cases. Why hadn't most people using the internet explode? I asked.

Adding another argument to his theory was a heart murmur isn't flakey skin. He explained to me that it wasn't the exact genetic disease or abnormality, but that these abnormalities make them venerable. Venerable to what? He handed me a printout of twenty pounds of code. What was it? I asked. It was the algorithm. Cool, so what's that have to do with people exploding?

He slapped me on the head. He explained there's lines in the code that located these abnormalities and it literally shake apart the genetic code. It all came together once he said that. It explained why they became viscera. It started at the genetic level and by the time they were ripped apart they were already goo. But there was a conclusion that formed in my head. Whoever made this algorithm did this?

Exactly. Jim said. He handed me a picture of a man wearing a light blue sweater and a smug smile. Who was this jerk off? Answer. Jeffrey P. Celine. I thought he was dead, but Jim said he was the junior. The senior was dead. The president of Cline Corps, a Silicon Valley company run by the Celine family.

Where do we go from here? I asked. He said Celine would be speaking at Tech Con in a week right here in Jim's town. We started planning and we were going to expose him to a large number of people. Not only his audience and supporters would be there, but also regular people. Schools and community members. It's all done for free. We can just walk in. It was easy.

We quickly became paranoid that it was too easy. What if they expect us? What happens once we drop this information bomb?

So we called the other three of the group. We came back together
to face this monster. Me and Jim were going to ask the questions
during the Q and A while two live streamed it and one watched it
from the parking lot in case we weren't allowed to leave.
The day came to packing five out of shape men into a van. We
drove in silence going through the plan over and over out loud
and in our heads. Like Trojans in a horse. We were going to blow
it up from the inside. We found a parking space on the out skits
of the arena. Jerry said good bye as the four of us went in.
We got there right on time. What he presented wasn't interesting.
Basically, it involved turning Jim's town into a tech center. A new
Silicon Valley. His plan was to diversify Jim's town and make it
state of the art. How he'd revitalize the town and finally replace
the dead industry with fancy tech jobs. The speech was so long.
Jerry texted me Tim's live stream was the floor, Tim had fallen
asleep. I tried to find him, but the crowd was so huge, it gave me
a panic attack.
It was three hours until we could ask our questions. Luckily, we
got close to the front of the line. As we waited, we watched on a
jumbotron. What stupid question these fat nerds are asking, but
aren't we doing the same. Except we were going to expose him,
so at least we had that. There were people screaming and I was
worried that they had also reached the same conclusions we had,
but they were mostly angry that the projects Celine proposed
would destroy their town. To which Celine replied all in the name
of progress.
I was next and held tightly to the print out of the algorithm Jim
had given me. I said I had information that links your coding to
the deaths of at least one hundred and fifty people. Mr. Celine is
using the algorithm to kill people by targeting genetic defects that
made them explode. A gasp takes over the audience.
He didn't react. He just sipped his water. Once he was finished,
he said I was correct. I asked why did you do that. His answer
was to wipe out twenty percent of the earth's population. That's
genocide. Maybe he said, but we're trying to save the planet
here and they got in the way. So we targeted people with genetic

defects to make our genetic code stronger. I'm a monster. The monster you need. To my surprised an explosion of applause followed deafening me.

As I was dragged away by security for asking more than one question. I yelled why do you want to kill us. He answered I didn't want to kill you because if I wanted to you would have exploded already. This was met with laughter and more applause. I couldn't believe it. He didn't even flinch. I was so defeated.

I was thrown out of the conference and then Jim came shortly after. Tim and Cody met us back at the van. There would be no imprisonment or torture. Only disappointment. We had the information on why people were exploding and everyone was fine with it.

The next day there wasn't even a mention of the conference in any news outlet. So we five came back together and wrote articles and spoke on podcasts about this but everyone said it was fake. The group tried for weeks, but to no avail. No one cared. The group splintered for the second and last time. Defeated again. They went forward with the plan to diversify Jim's town. It was a disaster. The rents sky rocketed and food became unaffordable. Jim and his wife became homeless. His wife went to live with her mother and he crashed on my couch. We tried to figure something out, but I had lost all interest after the conference and Jim was so depressed he wasn't really functioning. He slept on my couch for around three months and then disappeared. I didn't know what happened to him.

I stopped using the internet once I found out they were tampering with the algorithm to make it more efficient. I thought there might be a new batch of exploding people and I didn't want to find out I was one. I started to keep cash stashed everywhere. I tried not to use my phone. I barely left my house.

However, one last news article I read was about a lone gunman had snuck into the Celine Estate and attempted to kill Jeffery. I didn't click the article to find out if was Jim, but I hope he got what he wanted.

The Future is Bots

Jacob pulls up to the curb, softly hitting the sidewalk under the tightly packed snow. The suburban street is quiet. Rows of houses all look the same in the orange street light. He sits a moment before shutting off the car, looking over to Katie. On her phone flipping through her Twordly. Sitting sideways in the car seat, feet on the dash board. This is where Katie grew up and a month ago, he asked her to move in with him. She is obviously excited to be back home to have Christmas with her parents.

We're here.

I know. Not looking up from her phone, adding I felt it.

He fake laughs. Always on that phone. He just wants to smash it. Instead, he watches her giggle to herself. The shear glee on her face.

Look at this. Laughing sticking the phone too close to his face.

He grabs her wrist and watches a man jump out of a window. Landing on two feet, but regretting it. Legs bents in the opposite direction. There isn't any blood in the video. Just the man making

a funny noise. You should see your face. She laughs even harder.
He smiles. Funny.
Come on. She hits him.
What? It's funny.
Whatever. Going back to her phone.
He takes the keys out of the ignition and puts his hand on the
door handle, but when he goes to open it he notices something.
He squints and sees a large snowman, but as his eyes focus, he
realizes it's a man. Tie dye short sleeve shirt. Wearing sunglasses.
Looking right at the car. He taps Katie.
Do you see this?
What? She sits up. That guy.
Yeah.
What about him?
He's not wearing a coat.
So.
It's like ten degrees outside.
Maybe he's high.
Is he wearing sunglasses at night?
Maybe he likes to party.
Whispering Jesus fucking Christ, he opens the door.
When the light goes on Katie protests. Whoa, what are you do-
ing?
Getting out of the car. Walking to your parent's house. He
thought she'd be more excited to go, but all week she was trying
to get out of it. Setting up doctor appointments or needing him
to drive forty five minutes to see one of her stupid friend's DJ a
Christmas party. But, alas they all canceled. She convinced herself
that she needs to get her photography portfolio, she'd left it when
she moved into his place. There wasn't enough room and they
were hoping to find a bigger place. So far that plan has stalled.
He didn't understand why he was so excited. Maybe because since
moving in he might have regretted the decision. That's normal.
He loves her even though he didn't realize how annoying and
clingy she was. He also liked her parents. Normal people. Moder-
ate in every way.

Mom's not going to put the food on until we get there.
How do you know?
She messaged me on Twordly while you were parking. It alerted
her we were here.
Creepy. He gets out of the car and shuts the door.
She sighs. Putting her phone in her pocket. Pouting like a child.
Opening the door into the plowed snow and slamming the door.
Easy. Jacob locks the door. That guy is still there. Just standing
there.
I don't understand why you don't have Twordly. It makes every-
thing easier. You can do everything.
You know most of those people are bots, right.
You know most of those people are bot. She repeats mockingly.
Anyway, I had one remember. I told you. He watches that man,
who seems closer now. Jacob can make out his shirt tie dyed with
yellow lettering, Spring Fest 2009. I used to have that shirt.
What?
Nothing. Changing the conversation. What were we arguing
about again?
We were arguing about why you deleted Twordly.
Sounds about right. I deleted it because I was failing out of
school
You're not in school anymore Jakey. Get a another one.
No, it was stupid then. I can't imagine what it's like now.
Stupid. My parents have one.
Even your father, surprised, what do they do?
A lot actually. Looking for their accounts on her phone, they're
always on it. She shows him a picture of her as a child he'd never
seen with a caption reading miss my little girl.
Cute.
Weird. Pulling the phone back to her face. She doesn't post any-
thing I've done since. Like my career doesn't exist.
Well, when you moved out didn't you hate that your photography
was on the walls. What does your dad post?
Just stupid memes and photoshoped pictures of him on a desert
island.

Jacob laughs. Like dad jokes?

Worse. She scrolls and shows him a picture of a man at a party with captions saying they don't know I farted. He smiles. Jesus, you two deserve each other. Her face lights up again, so get an account.

No, I think I'll wait a while.

She hits him.

Hey. It's creepy.

Please, it just steals all your information.

And what does it do with it?

It's a surprise. She jokes.

Jacob smiles. He grabs her by the arm and walk down the sidewalk. She leans into him. He puts her arm around her, he wants to enjoy the stroll, but he keeps looking back at that guy. He starts to walk in their direction. He quickens the pace. They walk faster until Katie slips on a patch of ice. She laughs. He apologizes.

Help me up, snorting with laughter. His anxiety breaks. He turns back one more time. The man is gone. Thank God.

As they walk, he looks for that old fountain that was in her parent's yard. But none of the houses have it. Strangely, he can't tell the houses apart. They're all painted the same and a lot of them have eight feet of white fence.

Hey, did they redecorate?

They remodeled, but that was last month.

That was fast.

And mom and dad did it themselves.

Didn't your dad have a hip replacement surgery?

Yeah, I was joking with mom, she wants to kill him.

He carefully looks at the houses. That fountain in your front yard. I don't see it?

Oh yeah. Where is it? I can't tell these fences were never here before.

Did we go too far?

She looks down. The light from her phone illuminates her face. She looks up confused. It should be. She points to a house with the porch filled with boxes. There.

You sure?

Hold on. She texts. A moment later, her mother comes out of the house she pointed at. Told you.

You had to have your mother come outside.

It's been a long time.

They both begin to walk up to the house. Her mother hasn't waved or said hello yet. She is busy bring boxes into the house. When they get up to the house, Katie's mom doesn't even notice they're there. Jacob looks on the side of one of the boxes. Glassware. Fragile is printed on the side. She must have ordered this stuff online.

Mom, Katie sounding worried. Her mother still ignored her, Mom, she says louder.

She stops. Her mother looks up at her. Her expression goes from blank to overflowing with emotion. She finally greets them. Welcome home, baby. Her and Katie embrace. She waves at Josh. He waves back. Hey Dawn.

Katie pulls away from Dawn, Jesus, mom.

I guess I don't know my own strength. She smiles with too much teeth that makes Jacob uncomfortable.

Catching her breath, Mom. Jacob and I, noticed you got rid of that fountain.

She looks confused for a moment then hollowly laughs, that old thing. We threw it out.

Oh, Katie says, sounding hurt.

Anyway, come in out of the cold. She goads them inside. Jacob and Katie are astonished at what they walk into. Jacob thought when Katie said remodel, they may be painted or redid the ceiling. However, it looks completely different. When Jacob had helped Katie move the house was dim and cluttered with bills and books. The banisters and awnings were old and falling apart. Now it is bright and open. They had an old blue carpet from before they moved in. Removed and replaced by hardwood floors. The wood paneling replaced with a baby blue color with white framing at the floor and doors. Replacing Katie's portfolio are pictures of her father's photoshopped idea of a vacation. Jacob notices the heat. It snuck up on him. Even though it's winter, the house is muggy.

Wow, Dawn you did this all yourself.

She had some help. Her father appears from out of the living room.

Greg. Jacob shoots out his hand. He squeezes Jacob's hand too hard. Clenching his teeth in pain. You're not limping anymore.

Yeah, there is a pause, but he didn't follow up on Jacob's comment instead he says, it was really quick. Maybe his hip replacement is a touchy subject. He shrugs it off.

Come here, he says to Katie and she runs into his arms like a little girl. We've missed you.

I missed you too.

Let me take your coats, Dawn says. Katie and Greg unembraced. Jacob and her give her mother the coats. Greg leads them into the living room. Katie looks over the room.

Where's the Christmas tree?

It's in one of these boxes. Pointing to more boxes near the TV.

There's probably two. Your mom got one for free.

What happened to grandma's tree?

I don't know. Probably broken.

Katie is bewildered. Where are mom's books?

Not in my man cave.

Is that a joke?

No, he chuckles, she threw them out. Audiobooks. That's what she's into now.

Turning to Jacob. I thought mom hated audiobooks.

Dawn is always buying stuff. Replacing everything. Every day is a new experience.

Where's she buy all this stuff?

Twordly. I tell you it's got everything.

Does it? He askes curiously.

But Greg only shrugs and turns the TV up so loud the sound washes out giving Katie and Jacob an instant headache. This is my favorite show, he screams. They watch the blaring TV where people inspect hotels in tropical locations. They shame the management and then remake the hotel. Jacob is bored instantly, but he look over to Greg and he is captivated.

He look over at Katie. She isn't watching, she's curled up into a bowl, stiff and traumatized. Jacob reaches out and touches her. She pulls away. With his girlfriend upset, the blaring TV, and the heat Jacob stands up.

The bathroom is still in the same place?

Greg chuckles. It sure is. Eyes not leaving the TV.

Jacob just wants to go outside. It's freezing, but anything is a relief from this awkwardness. He walks through the boxes neatly stacked looking at the posters neatly framed. Interested, but after one or two admiring them, it becomes boring. Almost like a computer generated them. All photos of him are stock and posed weirdly that reminded him of that AI art.

He hears a noise, talking, then he realizes it's an audiobook. Greg said she loves audiobooks and sees in the kitchen, Dawn sitting on a stool an audiobook blurring out of her phone, which is pressed into her face. Grinning. Tapping her finger on the screen. He freezes. Shocked. After a moment she doesn't say anything. She doesn't even move. Just taps. No blinking. That smile. Who's it for. He keeps walking. Slowly. She doesn't move, only stares into the screen. He waves.

Hey, she barks.

Hi. She doesn't respond. Just going to the bathroom. He laughs uncomfortably.

I'm just buying stuff. She laughs. Can't get enough.

I guess so.

She is sitting by the sliding door. He turns and walks into the bathroom. Turning on the light and just standing in the middle of the tiled floor. After a few moments he starts to get impatient. Just walk outside. You're an adult. She probably won't care. But he remembers that grin. How long had she been like that. He sniffs the air. A trace of something in the air. It is a bathroom contradicting himself. He carefully lifts up the toilet seat. Nothing. He sits and cracks the window. The cool breeze feels so good. He didn't realize he was sweating.

He sees plastic wrap sticking out of the small closet. Curious, he opens the door. A heavy carpet falls on him bring him to the floor. He struggles to get out from under it when he sees eyes staring back at him. It's not a carpet. He sees a face. Dawn's face. Blood smearing all over the plastic. He lets out a scream. Instantly, there is a banging at the door.

Everything alright? Dawn asks.

Yup. Looking at her corpse. Water's a little cold.

It'll do that.

He finally wriggles out. He tears at the plastic roll until he reaches the skin and clothing beneath it. It's Dawn's body alright. But if she's there, who the hell is that. Does it matter? He needs to get Katie and leave. How? First, he's going to have to climb out of this window. He opens it and immediately stops too small for his frame. He sighs. He puts what's left of Dawn back in the closet and walks into the kitchen.

Everything alright? Dawn asks.

Yeah, I just got to make a phone call.

Oh, did you want to use this new goose down jacket I just bought.

He looks at the puffy orange winter jacket. No, I'll be fine with just this.

I've heard only good reviews.

Maybe later.

Not wanting to be rude, but she is really pushing the jacket. He opens the door and walks onto the well shoveled porch. He regrets it, forgetting he doesn't have a coat. It's calm. No sound at all. All the backyards are shoveled the same. Even the landscape of the yards. All have a tree with a tire swing. The same brown wooden porch. He takes a deep breath then he remembers Dawn's body and tenses up again. He starts to think, but his eyes focus on the tire swing in the yard. There's a figure by it. He strains his eyes. Maybe he's just seeing things, but then it steps into the light. Springfest 09 blazing across his chest. It's that guy.

Hello, Jacob says.

The man starts to run at him. The man is chanting something. Two syllables. The rhythm is so familiar. It reminds him of college. Then right before he is speared into the ground, he recognizes the chant. The word solidifies in his head. Spring fest. The man spits into his face and grabs Jacob by the throat. He tries to resist, but the man is so strong. He can barely keep him at bay. Jacob notices on the man's right arm the same stupid tribal tattoo he has. His grip loosens and the man's hands squeeze around his neck.

Struggling to not blackout. He sees the shovel and inches towards it until he knocks it into his hand. He hits the man with it. A black fluid drips out of the man's forehead. He hits him again, stabbing him in the face with the shovel's blade. This time the shovel easily rips into his neck revealing circuits and blinking lights. Jacob slams him one last time. The man topples off him and begins to shake.

What the fuck? He says still trying to catch his breath.

The black fluid frozen on his face. He goes over to inspect the body. He looks familiar. The haircut. The shirt. He hobbles over to the rubbery face. That's my face, he says to it. But he hasn't dressed like that since college. When he almost flunked out. When he deleted Twordly. He starts to hyperventilate. Confused about who could've done this. How could this have happened. That's what happened to Katie's parents.

He wanted to take my place. He pauses. But why?

There is a scream. The world suddenly becomes focused. Katie. The scream cuts out. He runs back into the house armed with only a snow shovel. Screaming as he enters the kitchen. It's quiet. Adrenaline pumping through his veins. Eyes darting there and here. Not a soul in the house. A door closes. The basement. He rushes to the door and throughs it open. Bounding down the dark creaking steps. When he turns the corner, he sees Katie lying unconscious. He finds her still breathing. He sighs in relief.

The tension snaps back when he notices a noise. There's that tapping again. He pivots and is greeted by Greg and Dawn. They don't seem interested in him, however. They are both emersed in their phones. Pressed into the faces. Tapping at their screens. He slowly reaches for Katie. Dawn lifts her head up and screams, I miss my little girl. Greg bellows, 99 percent off to a weekend in Bermuda. What a deal. They run at him full tilt. He closing his eyes and swings. He feels himself hit nothing air and then the ground. He quickly opens his eyes and they're gone. He turns and Dawn crutched on the wall drives at him. He closes his eyes and swings again.

He feels the shovel connect with her head. He opens his eyes and Dawns headless body is spurting black fluid. Still stand the headless body starts running around in a circle faster and faster until the spurting fluid is replaced with sparks. More and more until one spark catches and the reminisce of Dawn is engulfed in flames. Jacob watches for a moment at how beautiful it is, but Dawn's body falls over and the basement begins to go up in flames.

He needs to get Katie out of here, but just then Greg puts him into a head lock. Jacob flails around, trying to get Greg off him, but he only squeezes tighter. Not thinking, Jacob stands up and falls backwards. Greg's head is driven into the ground and that's when he feels Greg's grip loosen. Jacob picks up and throws Greg into the flames. Greg starts to swat at the flames, but the fires creep up his body. As Greg is engulfed in flames, Jacob grabs Katie and runs up the stairs. He hears Greg's burning body lumber up the stairs after them shout sales quotes, but once they are near the door they die down.

Slipping out the front door. Outside the raging flames heat Jacob's back. He turns and watches for a moment. He hears gun shots coming from the neighbor's house. He watches the muzzle flashes in the dim living room. Then seeing other houses catch fire and people screaming being chased down the icy street by replicas of themselves. It must be happening everywhere. He can't stop. Then goes to his car. Putting Katie in the passenger seat, strapping her in, and speeding out of the collapsing neighborhood.

The highway is empty. Jacob is still speeding as the sun comes up.

Speeding by curls of smoke rising from the towns dotting the off ramps. He hears Katie gasp as if she just came up from underwater. She looks around confused.

What...what happened?

I don't know.

My parents, she starts to weep, why would they do that?

They weren't your parents.

Then what were they?

I don't know. Robots or something.

She is silent. What?

I know how crazy it sounds, but they weren't humans.

He watches her put it all together in her head. They had superhuman strength.

Right.

My dad lifted me over his head. He was never that strong.

I don't know what they were.

Where are we?

On the highway.

Where are we going?

I don't know I was just driving.

She pulls out her phone. It's smashed. Shit. Can I barrow your phone?

For what?

Call the police.

Believe me, I'm sure they know. Motioning towards the plumes of smoke.

What?

Your house, neighborhood, he says slowly, it's all engulfed in flames.

What about my real parents?

They're dead. She starts to cry. He feels guilty, but he had to kill them. He should be crying.

Can I still barrow your phone? She pleads.

Sure, and he pulls it out of his pocket and hands it to her. She takes it and turns his back to him.

There is a long silence. The sun is up, but there is still no one on the road. The terror he felt has dissipated and he's driving at the speed limit. Maybe they got passed it. Katie hasn't moved in a while and he peers over. Her head is back on the head rest. Looking at his phone. He hears a noise a tapping. He thinks it's the car, but he turns and sees Katie with her phone pressed to her face. Tapping her finger on the screen. He contemplates pulling the car over.

The Chattering

Donny wakes up coughing again. Before his alarm. He reaches for the glass of water on his night stand only to find he is pinned to his bed. Like he melded with the mattress in the night. All his muscles are twitching madly. In the dark room, he sees wings fluttering all over his body. Butterflies he thinks, but then realizes it's a sleep paralysis episode. However, he has never had paralysis before. Only saw the effects on TV. That's when he hears a clicking. Like two rocks gentle clanking together. Then again. All around him. Over and over.

He calls for Stacey, his girlfriend lying next to him, but she doesn't stir under the confiscated blanket and pillows. He starts to shake his head and realizes he can move, but he's stuck like Velcro.

He rolls back and forth, but the grip doesn't loosen. He just decides to sit up. The bed sheet tears and pieces of it come with him. His mother won't be happy about that. The rip wakes up Stacey. Her voice tells him to knock it the fuck off. He ignores it.

He tries to pull the sheet off, but it's firmly stuck to his skin. He rummages around for the lamp string, finds it, and pulls.

He sighs. It's much worse than sleep paralysis. He is covered in mouths. Mouths without lips or tongues only crooked rows of teeth growing from his skin gnashing and chewing at the air. He can't hear anything because the mouths keep clicking. He just watches the mouths for a while wondering why him.

Turn off the light. Stacey says from the pile of blankets and pillows.

Sorry. He obliges. Listening to them click loudly. Feeling them twitch all over.

What's that noise?

I think it's the radiator.

You're going to have to tell your mother about that.

Fine. He says trying not to get into a fight so early in the morning.

The whole thing depresses him. Another terrible thing upon a pile of terrible things. He imagines walking onto a highway and becoming spattered on a mac truck's bumper. The whole town would say look at all these teeth this local loser had in his mouth. It wouldn't be on the nightly news. He wouldn't even be a foot-note. That's how terrible his life is. Maybe suffering is better.

The alarm cuts the silence of his thought. The sun slants through the bedsheet curtains. He can still hear the clicking over the alarm. Stacey reaches over him and shuts off the alarm. He de-cides to get ready for work. Gently getting out of bed this time so not to wake Stacey. Making it to a standing position as the mouths on the soles of his feet bite into the carpeted floor. Slow-ly making his way to the bathroom.

While standing in the shower the mouths remind him of turkeys in the rain. Opening and closing. The shower water goes in, but doesn't come out. Donny doesn't feel the mouths swallow or the water dribble out. Where did the water go? Looking at the mouth in the palm of his hand. Opening and closing. Looking into a deep abyss. Does it empty in his body? Who cares answering his own question. The clicking is becoming more and more annoying. Just clicking in no particular pattern. There's no escape from it. How can his life continue? He's not even sure if this would constitute disability.

The shower door opens and Stacey gets in. Standing in front of him. Hogging the water. The clicking bounces off the plastic walls of the shower. Her butt grazes his lower leg and she jumps as one of the mouths pinches her.

What the fuck? She yells. Pivoting to meet him, she sees he's covered with mouths. She slumps in disgust. Her lip curls with frustration. What the fuck is this? She says disappointed.

I don't know. He says. I just woke up with them.

Is it like the flu or something?

I don't think so. He answers.

Asshole. She opens the door and walks out.

He wants to say sorry, but realizes there's nothing to be done. So he reaches for the soap, but it quickly gets chewed up by the teeth. Sick of these teeth he shuts off the water. Trying to find a relaxing way to get dressed he sit on the toilet. He finds himself being pinched and bitten trying to put on his shirt. When he finally manages to pull his clothes on, the mouths bite down pulling his clothes taught. Then relaxing. Tiny holes begin to form on his clothing. I just bought this shirt. He explains to the mouths, but there is no discussion.

Constantly pulling and tugging pieces of shirt and pants out of the mouths he finally makes it upstairs. Sitting at the table sipping coffee are his mother and Stacey.

His mother turns. What's this?

He shrugs.

Well, it better not ruin the interior of my car. She goes back to her coffee. Just got it redone. He pours himself a cup and his mother gets up. Well, we should probably get going. She pushes the auto start. He hears the old minivan roar from the driveway. Black smoke rising.

But I just made myself a cup.

Do you want a ride or not. We're leaving now. He looks at his coffee and pours it down the sink.

You could have just put it in the frig.

It would've gotten cold.

That's what the microwave is for.

Grosse.

He follows her and Stacy to the dented green minivan. He tries to grip the door handle, but the mouth in his palm makes it difficult. Constantly opening and closing, but eventually after both his mother and Stacey scold him he uses both hands to open it. His mother tells him to sit with his arms cross as to not mess up her newly upholstered seats. She talks nonstop driving to avoid the main roads they wind through cul de sacs and lightly treed areas until popping out at the convenient store Stacey works. Stacey awkwardly kisses him on the forehead. She opens the siding door and disappears into the parking lot.

Once Stacey leaves there is a pause in his mother's motoring mouth. He thinks she going to tell him to see a doctor. He is correct.

You should go see Dr. Howard again.

I don't think he takes my insurance.

Oh please, and can't you stop the clicking.

I don't have any control.

Of course, you don't. Donny, this can't be healthy. Who knows it might have been the vaccine. Did you think of that?

You and Stacey got vaccinated and this didn't happen to you.

You have a weak constitution.

Oh fuck off mom. The car stops abruptly and Donny's head hits the dashboard. Shit. Rubbing his head.

Fuck off? How dare you? Get out.

What?

Get out. Going to talk to me like that. You can walk.

Fine.

He takes a step onto the side of the road as she drives off with the door still open. He can see the general store. Grateful he didn't tell her to fuck off when Stacey got dropped off. That would've been quite the walk. He enters the sliding doors to work.

Everyone looks at him not only because the visible mouths reaching out to bite them, but also the nonstop clicking of the teeth. It doesn't help that the mouths grab anything within a few inches. Ripping bags of candy and knocking items off the shelf. Which is not so bad, it only really slows his pace to clock in. The manager Jerry walks by him and they both wave to each other. Then he hears a whoa. He sighs and waits for Jerry to scold him as well.
What's on your arms?
Mouths.
Mouths. Are they contagious?
I don't think so.
Well, you're going to need to cover them because I don't want them biting the customers.
Cover them with what?
Go in back. There's a box labeled work shirts. Get a long sleeve shirt. Once your shift is over return it.
Alright. Donny starts to walk away.
And try not to snag any merchandise on your way there. Donny waves sarcastically.
Muttering about how he doesn't need this stupid job. He looks through the box of work shirts between the bleach and other poisons. Looking through each shirt trying to find the one without too many stains or holes. He finally finds a red one and puts it on. The sleeves on his forearms immediately twitch with mouths chewing through the fabric. He shrugs and goes back to work. He walks out of the employees only area into the store. He walks up and down the aisle pretending to work. Ignoring the twitching beneath the shirt and the customers eyeing him. Sooner or later he sees Jerry coming down the aisle asking what he's doing. He thought organizing is a good enough answer, but Jerry doesn't seem to agree. Jerry hands him the price gun and makes him check the prices in the store.
Using the price gun as slowly as possible, Donny gets a tap on the shoulder. He turns and it's a little old lady.
Hello, sir. I was wondering if you have left handed scissors for children?

Aisle four. He points in the aisle's direction turning back around.
No, I checked there. They're not there.
We must be out.
Can I speak to your manager? He looks around to figure out where Jerry could be. He hears her gasp. Her face is looking at his shirt. He looks down and the mouths have eaten right through his two shirts.
Shit. He says and that's when she starts to scream.
Pointing she says, what is wrong with you?
What? No. It's not contagious.
She doesn't stop screaming, so he puts the price gun down and runs away. He finds an empty aisle and tries to inspect the damaged shirts. The mouths completely ruined both shirts. They even chewed through the sleeves. He looks down and his pants are mangled too. A pretty young woman in a light blue dress comes down the aisle.
Excuse me, are you on break?
No. He says hoping she ignores the rags he's wearing. How can I help you?
I need someone with a key to get this Advil. Pointing toward the liquid gels.
Well, you're in luck. Jiggling his keys. He unlucks the liquid gels. As he turns to hand the small box to her, he hears a loud tear.
What the fuck? She screams. Her dress most have gotten caught in one of the mouths and was ripped off her body. She isn't wearing anything underneath. Holding herself.
Oh, my God. He says in shock. I'm sorry. Reaching towards her.
Give me my dress back creep. He pulls her dress out of the mouth that snatched it.
Sorry. Holding up her dress. She grabs it.
Where is your manager? He gets on his tip toes to find Jerry.
Never mind, I'll find him myself. Slipping the dress back on and angrily stomping off.
Later, in Jerry's office. Jerry sighs. Ok, so she isn't pressing charges.
Is that good?

Very good. I told her it was a medical condition. You are going to
have go to a doctor to cover our asses.
Donny sinks into his seat. Fine.
Great. Let me know and we can schedule you in. There is an awk-
ward pause. Jerry looks up at him. Anything else?
No.
Great. You can go home now. He takes his phone and starts call-
ing his mother.
You can do that outside. He leaves Jerry's office.
Waiting for his mother to pick him up he leans against the wall.
He can't get comfortable because the hard teeth scrape against
the brick. Continuing to clicking and twitching. It's maddening.
He tries squatting, but the teeth from the back of his calf bite
and lock in with the other teeth from his upper leg. He just ends
up standing upright. Breathing in exhaust from the cars coming
and going. The air has a yellow tint to it. There is a smell in the
air like a camp fire. Those forests must still be burning. Maybe
it's the food processing plant making a new cereal. The thoughts
don't get answered instead just linger and are forgotten.
Finally, his mom pulls into the parking lot. Two rows away. He
starts walking towards the car, but she gets out.
I just need to get something. I'll be right back.
Are the doors unlocked? She walks too quickly to answer. Fuck.
He mutters.
Going over to the passage side and tugging the handle. Nope.
He says to the busy parking lot. Squeezing himself between his
mother's car and the car right next to it. The teeth rubbing on the
hot plastic sheen of the green minivan. He moves around the car
to let people into adjacent vehicles and wait until they drive away.
He hears the car beep. She unlocked it.
Sorry. Her arms full of bags. He goes to get in. Wait. Wait. She
pulls a large plastic tarp and puts it on the front seat. How Hu-
miliating. There you go. He hops in. My God, look at you. She
says not paying attention to road. Those mouths ate right through
your shirt. Good thing you're going to the doctor. He'll know
what to do.

Can I have his number? I need to schedule an appointment.

I already made it. Tomorrow at 10am. He is kind of pissed she made an appointment already, but it is more a relief. Maybe all of this might be almost over.

Donny spends the rest of the day bumps into everything counter, doors, and Stacey, who is not enthused, but after three times she starts to laugh and hit him playfully. His mother watches in disgust as the two of them find things for the mouths to chew. Sausages, rock, whatever they found the crooked yellow teeth could bite throw it with ease. Later Donny leans against a wall his mother always complains about and the mouths twitch and pulse and after a half hour he falls into the other room. Stacey and him laugh and laugh.

The next day Stacey, his mother, and him get into the car. He can't shut the door right away and his mother curtly says, Come on. I want this day to be over with.

You didn't have any fun yesterday.

No, and it's not going to be fun today. She starts to engine and goes whizzing to the doctor's office. Walking in the parking lot his mother quickly gets in front of them. She doesn't hold the door and he watches her check him in. He wonders if she's embarrassed by him. This is worse than her having a son and his girlfriend living in her basement. He used to be a loser, but now he's a freak.

Leaving Stacey and his mother in the waiting room with old magazines, he follows Dr. Howard to an examine room.

Hello Donny, Long time no see.

Well, yes. My new job has terrible insurance.

That's life. He pauses. Now your mother said something about a rash.

Not exactly.

Let's take a look. Donny takes his shirt off. Dr. Howard hmms and makes pensive sounds. Are they all over your body or only on your arms and chest.

All over.

And they have throats.

Yeah, but I don't know where they go. Donny says. Dr. Howard doesn't say anything for a long time just staring at the mouths. My mom thinks it's from the vaccine. Donny says to break the tension.
No. It isn't.
Why not?
Because vaccines don't make people grow mouths. They give you clots or heart attacks or autism. Not this type of physical side effect.
Are you sure?
I read the studies.
Well, what the hell is it?
I don't know. He starts write. We'll run some tests and see how they've grown and where the mouths end. Who knows you might be budding.
What's that?
A form of asexual reproduction.
Confused he asks, Am I the man or woman?
Let's find out.
Dr. Howard and the nurses take tissue samples, blood samples, and x rays. They shine flashlights down into the mouths. After three hours Dr. Howard returns to Donny's room.
I've looked over your tests.
And.
Inconclusive.
What? How? Dr. Howard just shrugs. Even the x rays.
Yeah, the x rays didn't pick up where the mouths go.
What about the samples?
Normal. You're actually in great health.
Donny slumps. Great. There's no medication or cream.
Oh no. I have no idea what's going on.
Thanks. He starts walking towards the door.
Let me know if anything changes.
Sure.
He meets Stacey and his mother in the lobby. His mother is dis-appointed at the results. They all go home. Donny depressed he

can't go back to work. He thinks about getting a second opinion, but the bill from Dr. Howard comes back and his insurance isn't going to pay for the visit. That idea slips out of his mind. However, the days following are better. His mother buys mats for him to sit on, so the mouths won't chew throw the house immediately. Stacey starts to take hours off from work to spend time with him. Even his mother starts being nicer to him. Him, Stacey, and Her sit on the couch after everyone gets home and laugh at car crashes and people getting hit in the face with broads. These next few days are actually alright.

One day he finds himself alone in the house. His mother and Stacey are both working. He looks outside and sees it's a beautiful day. He moves a mat outside to bathe in the sun. He starts to doze off. He awakes up to something pawing his chest. He looks up and sees the neighbor's cat, Fluffy, kneading at his chest. The cat is neither fluffy nor cute. Quite fat and mean. He wants to shoe it away, but he thinks once it gets bit it will stop.

However, he watches the cat knead his side. Fluffy screams. Must have gotten bit. He smiles. Donny sees the cat's paw is caught in one of the mouths. The mouth doesn't let Fluffy go. Fluffy just keeps making an awful piercing noise. Tugging. Trying to get free. He watches Fluffy being pulled into himself. The mouth swallowing the cat slowly. He watches awestruck as the cat disappears. The cat's screams are cut off.

He jumps up and shakes off the mat. Gliding over his body trying to find where the cat went inside of him. He can't find any evidence. The cat just vanished into a bottomless pit. He starts to feel the mouths pulsate. He hears the clicking not just of one mouth, but all of the mouths, the teeth gnashing is sequence. They all bend in ninety-degree angles. There is a gurling noise from within him. The mouths gapping open. Parts of the cat are regurgitated from every mouth. The wet chunks spit out dangling from a few of the teeth. The stink is overwhelming. Then from one mouth a spout of blood comes out. He hopes that's it, but then sheets of blood shoot out in streams from every mouth. It's not cat's blood, but his own. He starts to sink into himself.

Deflating, feeling his skin gently lay against guts and bones. The bloodless body can no longer take the weight and falls to the ground. The last thing Donny hears is clicking of teeth.

This Company is a Prison

He had the dream again. Trying to forget it. Trying to focus on work. But no matter how hard he tries he can't get Veronica's broken face out of his head. And how he beat her. Shaking it off. Another story for Dr. Gibbson. Trying to laugh, but the joke falls flat. He starts to type, going back to work. Hopefully, it will help him forget, but he's been writing, deleting, and rewriting the same paragraph for a few hours now. He tells himself that Veronica isn't that bad. He doesn't understand why his unconscious would target her. Sure she's nitpicky, but they don't even work in the same department or on the same floor. The Editing Department while he's in the Proposal Department. Since telework was implemented, she's never in the office. Why does this dream of killing her keep persisting? She does remind him of someone he used to know, but can't remember who.

Going back to the proposal for Celine Co.'s new initiative to get federal contracts to fund experimental prison programs to drop the recidivism rate. The initial proposal of putting a chemical into the felons drinking water to become reformed members of society failed to gain traction. There was a problem with the solubility of the substance into water. They would put too much and make people vegetables or too little and people would go and commit the same crimes. His solution is to put an implant at the base of the inmates' neck. He has been assured that it's minor surgery. According to the surgeons, there's no scars and apparently the chemical agent needed to react with the body is in the process of the breakdown of food. This is how it will replenish itself. No needles, prescription, or additional surgeries.

He had to read many scientific journals and books to grasp what these doctors were talking about. After months, he finally finished the first proposal. His first pitch was a week ago and there were plenty of edits. Especially from Veronica. Interrupting during the pitch. Pointing out misspelling and spacing problems on the PowerPoint. Then he read through her notes. The most memorable: I don't know what this mean? Is this against the law? This should be a semicolon. Even after having it toned down. He went back and rewrote parts and put in language that had to be added for legal reasons and here it sits as an attachment in the email. Everyone is waiting for the presentation tomorrow. He just needs to send it. If it isn't perfect, he'll have to spend all night and maybe the morning working on it. Fuck it. He whispers in his cubicle. He hits send. He feels oddly better. Looking at his computer, he realizes his appointment with Dr. Gibson is an hour away. Leaving the office down the windowless corridor with a myriad of art pieces that were supposed to be substitutes the natural light. They were supposed to move too. However, he never saw it. The only picture that stands out to him one with two birds flying in the opposite direction. He recognizes it because Dr. Gibbson has a painting similar, only the two birds are flying in the same direction. He always thought it was strange that the place he worked and his therapist had paintings by the same artist.

I'm really worried about this dream.

Why, do you think you'll actually act on it?

No, it's just strange. I don't even know this woman, but for some reason I hate her.

Well, you said she reminded you of someone.
Right.
Do you know who?
No, I can't even put my finger on who she reminds me of.
It could be that she's the only bump in the road to getting this
proposal approved. You're just putting all of your anger and frus-
tration on her.
Maybe.
Have you spoken to her?
Not really. The only time I really see her is during these meetings.
There's no hanging out at a bar after work?
Yeah, but I'm too busy.
You should go. If she's there maybe talk to her. Who knows you
might like her.
Shouldn't I stay away from her.
Why?
I don't know. Maybe you're right.
Would you just try it.
Fine.
After leaving Dr. Gibson with a bizarre promise. He takes the
subway home and when he gets above ground again his whole
block is torn up. There are orange cones and yellow caution tape
all around. He weaves through the mess into his building where
he sees the doorman.
What happened?
Water main burst.
Can I use the water?
The maintenance says there should be enough in the tank to take
a shower.
When will it be fixed?
They're working on it now. They estimate it'll be done in the
morning.
Great.
He goes up the elevator to the fourteenth floor and goes into
his apartment. He immediately goes to his frig and gets his water
purifier and fills it up. He checks his email to see if there are any

edits to his proposal tomorrow. Surprisingly, there isn't. He swells
with pride. Not having anything to do he watches a little TV and
then goes to bed. Saving the water for a shower before he goes to
work in the morning.

That night the dream was falling leaves. Veronica was there. He
wasn't beating her, but enjoying her. Her name was Emily. He
wakes up refreshed. He feels like the slump he was in was over.
He goes to the bathroom and turns the shower knobs. The pipes
rattle and hot water shoots out from the head. Something going
right. Putting his head under the water, today is going to be a
good day. He only gets a minute or two when the shower cuts
off. He is surprised, but expected this to happen. He gets out
and makes coffee. He gets the water from the tap and when the
machine starts to brew the coffee, he remembers he has purified
water in the frig. Oh well and continues making the coffee.
Walking up to the Celine Co. It's a giant building dominating the
skyline. He becomes more nervous. He tries to clamp it down.
He keeps telling himself he is going to nail it. However, he knows
psyching himself out like a sort of football player isn't what
works. Only a quiet confidence will get him through this. He goes
to his desk and looks over his notes and the power point. He
goes through it, so fast he has a few more hours until his presentation. He surfers the internet watching only funny videos as to
not put himself in a slump.

When it's time to present the proposal, he goes into the conference room fifteen minutes early and sets up the projector to make
sure everything is in work order. He doesn't want any hiccups.
People start piling into the room. Taking seats around the big
oval table and seats against the wall. He glances up and see Veronica sitting nearest the door. Maybe it's because he drank too
much coffee this morning, but her figure is sharper than everyone
else. Her skin and clothing are vivid and bright then the figures in
the dark.

Once everyone has found a seat he starts, good morning, everyone. I'm going to be talking today about the modified proposal
for prison reform. You should have received my email yesterday

with the proposal and the science used to back it up. The room
is silent and he begins going through the slides and punctuating
the main points. Even though he looks around the room his gaze
always falls back to Veronica. As if she's the fulcrum upon which
he spins. His mind wishes to explore this idea, but he quickly puts
it back on track without a stutter. Finally, he asks if there are any
questions. The dark room is silence. Alright, thank you and have
a nice day.

People start to get up and chit chat. He stands there for a few and
then starts to pack. Jerry, his department head comes up to him,
shaking his hand, great job. We're bound to get that contract.

Thank you, sir.

We're all going out to the bar across the street. You should come.

Sure. I'm going to pack and I'll meet you there.

Great, he grins.

He packs up and watches the parade of his coworkers move
across the giant glass wall like a 1920s cartoon short. Happy and
laughing marching to get drunk. Through the white buttoned up
shirts and dull green dresses he sees Veronica. She is laughing at
something then she glances over to him. He quickly looks away
and when he looks back up her gaze is unbroken. She smiles. He
smiles back. Then her face is obscures in the rivalry and quickly
moves to the elevator leaving him in the quiet vacant office. He
locks all the material in his desk and goes to the bar alone.

The party is already going on with people ordering drinks and
dancing. Trying to get loosened up. Someone yelling at him to
get a drink. Without argument he orders a beer. Sitting at the bar
watching people dance and gyrate to the loud music. He looks
over and he sees Veronica poking her plastic straw into her drink.
Taking Dr. Gibson's advice, he approaches her.

Hey Veronica.

She looks up and smiles. Hey, how are you?

Much better now that presentation is over.

I bet. Seemed hard.

Parts of it.

Like what?

The science.
Oh yeah, her eyes brighten, I could hardly follow it. She pauses.
But I thought you did a good job at explaining it.
Thanks. I'm happy to hear that it made sense.
So are they really going to put things in prisoners' brains.
If we get the funding.
Sounds awful.
Yeah, but it's probably going into trails, if that. Mostly I think
once we get funding, they'll test it on animals first.
That's worse.
It sure is.
Do you like animals?
Yeah, I grew up with cats and dogs.
Really, which did you like better?
Probably dogs.
Me too. Just then someone bumps into her spilling her drink. He
hands her some napkins.
Where'd you get the dress?
You like it? I found it at a thrift store.
Very bright. She smiles.
That broke the ice and they start to talk about themselves freely.
It feels like they're old friends. As if they'd known each other for-
ever. As the conversation becomes more comfortable the more,
they drink. Within a short time talking they are making out at the
bar. A crowd gathers collectively saying, oh.
Let's go somewhere else.
We could go back to my place.
Sure. Do you have a car?
No, but I live two subway stops away.
She smiles, great.
Once in the privacy of his apartment they take off their clothes
and the curves of her body are familiar. As if both of them are
meant to fit together. The movements and noises almost are a
comforting memory. Now mangled together they fall fast asleep.
He slips into sleep looking forward to the morning.
However, that isn't what happens. He jolts awake. He has a

violent dream. He can't remember what it is about. All he remembers from the dream is Veronica's scream. He sits up. Veronica isn't there. A sense of dread comes over him. He hears the pipes in the bathroom bang together then stop.

Veronica's silhouette in his doorway. Hey, is there something wrong with your shower?

Oh shit. He forgot about the water main. The water main burst. I guess they still haven't fix it. Sorry.

It's fine. He couldn't see her face, but he could tell she is disappointed. I think I'm going to go home.

He looks at his phone. 3:30 am. Alright, you want me to walk you to the subway?

No, I'll be fine. Her voice sounds hurried. Bye. The door closes. He sits up in bed thinking what a strange situation. A sense of guilt starts to form. It spins around in his head for a while and then he drifts off into sleep again. The alarm blares and he opens his eyes. He wants the take a shower or wash his sheets, but he can't do any of that. He gets dress and leaves the apartment hoping the issue of the water main is fixed before he gets home. Walking out of the subway, he looks at the skyline and doesn't recognize it. The Celine Co. building, which should be towering over the other building is gone. The building in front of him is stumpy from what he remembered from yesterday. Lost among the silhouette against the rising sun. He thinks he still isn't fully awake. He hasn't had a cup of coffee or anything. Once walking through the revolving doors, he needs to take a second to realize all the grey modern paneling is replaced by scaffolding with exposed brick and mortar. That was fast. They must have started a remodel during the night. Confused, he forgets about it once he reaches the elevators.

The elevator doors open and he walks down the corridor he'd walk down for three years and all of the paintings were gone. Replaced by doors. What the hell was going on? For a second, he thinks he might be in the wrong build. Where's that painting with the two birds? He has to stop to take it all in. He worries he is losing his mind, but he looks down the corridor and can see

his desk. Too much stress. Maybe he needs to go on a vacation. That's what he'll do. Once he gets to his desk, he'll request a week of leave.
At his desk, finishing his leave request. Don comes up to him.
Hey, Don.
Hey, how's it going?
I'm fine. Some remodeling. Thumbing towards the exposed brick.
Don looks confused. Remodeling?
Yeah, the exposed brick. All the paintings.
It's been like this for at least a year. He pauses, and what painting?
Oh, I think on the second floor. There were some. Making something up on the fly.
Oh, I don't know anything about that but, great presentation yesterday.
Thanks.
I think you convinced the board to take another look at the prison project. At this news, his anxiety breaks.
Great.
Yeah, big things are coming. He knocks at his cubical and leaves. He couldn't help, but smirk. He wants to tell someone, but he doesn't think anyone is in the building. Checking his email. There is nothing new. Looking to check if there are any meetings. Nothing. He shrugs. Lazy day. He gets up and goes to the water cooler. From a far he sees Veronica getting a drink. He walks up to her.
Hey. He says awkwardly.
Oh hey. How's it going?
I just wanted to apologize for the water. I forgot.
No problem. She turns and starts to walk away seemingly still upset. He doesn't understand why.
Emily.
Who's that? She turns to him. You don't even remember my name.
No.
I knew it. She laughs. That water main story was a lie to get me out of your apartment?
No, I meant it was a mistake.

She walks right up to his face. Listen. I'm not a whore, poking at him, and I'm only going to tell you this once, he tries to apologize again, but she keeps interrupting, you stay away from me.

As she starts to walk away he says, Veronica, he grabs her arm and twists. He feels the crack of cartilage. She screams in pain. She falls to the floor dramatically. He lets her go. Sorry. Then looking down at how pathetic she looks something comes over him and he grabs her by the cheeks. But when he goes to scream in her face, he finds not Veronica or Emily, but another woman. Someone he's never met. Terrified he lets go the woman fall back to the floor. Sorry, sorry.

What's going on here? A voice interrupts. He turns and something hits him on the head. He tumbles to the floor. He feels blood slide down the side of his face. Veronica. Falling leaves. Emily. The warm touch on a cold day. The pain comes before he wakes up. Opening his eyes all he can see is a blinding spot light. He tries to shield his eyes, but finds he is restrained. A dark figure comes into view. His eyes begin to focus and he slowly starts to see that it's Dr. Gibson.

Well, that was disappointing.

What?

We were about to release you, but now we can't.

I don't…

Understand, Dr. Gibson finishing his thought. I don't suppose you do. Maybe we let you off the chemical too soon. That pipe bursting was a problem.

What chemical?

The chemical we put in your drinking water.

Like those prisoners?

You are the prisoner.

The room pauses. But I'm for Celine Co. I'm a free man.

You guys really hit him on the head too hard this time. Dr. Gibson says to someone he can't see.

Sorry to break the news, but you're a murderer.

What?

Remember. Emily or what was her name in the simulation.

Veronica?

You killed her. You joined this program to see if you could divert your sentence.

His past is coming back to him slowly. He remembers vaguely what he is saying. Falling leaves. Her broken face. The scream.

Those dreams. I didn't kill her this time.

True, but you broke the actress' arm.

I said I was sorry. He starts to weep.

Sorry, isn't justice.

Are you going to send me back to prison?

You haven't been paying attention at all. He is confused about Dr Gibson's statement. However, Dr. Gibson disappears and reappears with the implant he talked about during his presentation.

No, no prison for you. Just minor surgery.

Message Boards are Sentiant

I knew Charlie was going to kill me long before he and his horde started assassinating and burning builds. The last time I saw him he told me so. It was a rough patch in my life, Brittany, my girlfriend left and I was alone in my empty apartment when who came crawling up my wall. Hairless, translucent skin with blue veins throbbing. Out of his lipless mouth he prophesized my time would come. He pointed his shaved down fingers to the bone and told me he'd do it himself.

Needless to say, I stopped going outside. I started to work from home. I bought a security system with cameras and locked for my windows and doors. Got my food delivered and lastly, I bought a gun. Pointing it loaded around my apartment and watching videos of where the safety is and how to store it proper.

Within a month I hardly recognized myself. That's when they assassinated their first person. A local city council member, Kacey Schmit. I never heard of her, but they apparently didn't like her. The horde of monsters Charlie was a part of didn't shoot her or blow her up or anything like that. They just ripped her limb from

limb and hung her torso in her living room with her own entrails.
The police found her fiancé in a similar way. Just not on display.
That incident started the ball rolling: killing higher level politi-
cians, burning farmlands, and destroying the power grid. It was
international. The news covers all the similar crimes happening,
not only in the west, but in South America, Asia, and Africa. People didn't know whether to cry or cheer considering the carnage
of the death and disrupting people's way of life. It was hard to
get people to deliver my food and the internet stopped working.
I've been isolated for about two months. Charlie's prophecy could
come true at any moment. It's hard to believe whatever this is all
started because me and Charlie started a group on Twordly.
We were unemployed and bored. Just out of college with nothing
to lose. We heard people were making money creating message
boards on Twordly, a social media site, I already had an account,
but Charlie was hesitant. He said they'll sell our information
to the CIA. I told him that they probably already had enough
information. He thought was a good point, so we became group
admins.
Our message board was about weird stuff UFOs, Conspiracy
Theories, and strange art. At first, we would post other people's
memes and content which almost got us kicked off the platform.
Apparently, the creators of those memes and things threatened to
sue Twordly, so we removed all the posts. Then we became content creators. Charlie and I thought this would be an easy buck,
but now we had to actually work. At first it was memes and then
we started writing and shooting fake news videos. It was so hard
and I wanted to quit every day, but looking back it was probably
the best time in my life.
However, it was not the best time of Charlie's life. When we
started making money, it was great because we could hire more
people. Not professionals, but people who were on the message
board. They posted content too, so we decided to make them
admins. I thought it was great because we didn't have to do all the
work, but Charlie wasn't into it. He had the idea that we could
change people's lives. That this message board with its reach

could change the world. I laughed and he screamed at me. I had never seen him like this. He was rabid like a zealot.

To calm him down I asked him if he could give me an example and he showed me the memes and content created by a user named, Al Goryhtm, funny. This guy's content wasn't funny rather it was very serious. There were posts about billionaire elites poisoning food and everything else, which was pretty boiler plate. However, the videos that worried me were the strange occult rituals and live human sacrifices all tied together with an ideology of conquering the world. Things that would made my skin crawl. Charlie didn't see it like that. He was hooked on what this Al Gorythim guy was saying. He even wanted to make him an admin to the board. He was so hysterical all I could say was we'll put it to a vote.

I looked up this Al Gorythim on our page. I found him quickly. His profile picture was a picture of the owl god Moloch. I looked at his profile, but there wasn't anything there. He wasn't following anyone. There wasn't even uploaded of his videos or memes. Maybe this account is a bot. I did a reverse IP to see if I could see where he lived, but there was a server error.

I was going to alert the other admins about this strange account when I saw that Al Gorythim was already an admin for the message board. I asked other admins if there was a vote and they'd said no. I tried to remove him, but I couldn't do that either. Frustrated, I went to confronted Charlie.

He lived a block away from me. I knocked on the door and his mother answered. I was cordial and his mother asked me how my family was. I said fine, but then she asked if I could talk to Charlie, maybe even hangout with him. Go to a movie or something. I said sure. She invited me in and I went down to the basement where Charlie was.

I hadn't been down there in months. It was a regular twenty-year-olds room filled with clothes, video games, and electronics scattered around the room. However, now it was dark and unwelcoming. The only light was from the illuminated computer screen. I said his name to the darkness and there was movement.

Then there was light. Charlie looked pale and gaunt. At first, I thought he'd given himself a bad haircut, but looking closer his hair was falling out in clumps. I could make out a clump here and there in the dim light. He lost thirty pounds and hadn't been sleeping. His baggy clothes were torn and stiff from being worn too long.

 After the initial shock of his appearance, I asked if he added that Al Gorythim guy to the admin. He said no. I didn't believe him, so I pressed the issue, but he insisted he didn't. He didn't even know he was an admin. I asked him what he knew about this guy and he shrugged. I asked him again and he said something strange. That they were talking to each other and apparently this guy wasn't a real person, but the algorithm itself. Charlie goes on saying how he's being rewired. Transcending. Evolving. I didn't think to ask into what?

I was shocked. My friend had gone insane. I changed the conversation immediately and asked if he wanted to go out for a coffee. He said no, but I said I would pay and he agreed. Driving to the closest coffee shop Charlie was skidish and he kept talking about Al Gorythim. How amazing it was that artificial intelligence could evolve to be a leader. Have plans. His philosophy of world domination. Murdering elites and burning food supplies. Needing soldiers to carry out the plan. How the algorithm chose him. It sounded like gibberish to me.

At the coffee shop, Charlie kept looking around. I asked if he was ok and he told me that the algorithm was everywhere. It wasn't just our message board, but hundreds, even thousands. I wasn't going to get any answers from him in this state. So I just let him talk until I had enough and yelled at him in the nice chairs in the coffee shop. There was no plan. Someone's just hacked our message board. I called him insane. It made the whole place look at us.

I was embarrassed. I felt even worse when Charlie stood up and told me to go fuck myself. He left the coffee shop and when I chased after him, he was nowhere to be found. So I went home and wrote to Twordly's admin. The response I got back was not encouraging. They said there was no record of the account and couldn't see the posts or admin page I was talking about.

If I couldn't delete this account or even report it I could at least save Charlie, so I reported him. That went through and I decided I needed a break from the internet anymore for a couple of days. One day I went grocery shopping. That's when things went from strange to scary. In the sauce aisle, I was trying to find a healthy vodka sauce when I saw something out of the corner of my eye. I looked left and there were hooded figures, so I turned right and there were even more.

I asked nervously if I could help them and one of them was Charlie. He had removed his hood and he looked even worse. Completely hairless and bloodshot eyes. He'd ground his teeth into sharpened fangs. He walked right up to my face. Telling me I made a mistake in trying to remove him. I wanted to tell him I was sorry, but he turned and the mob left. It took a moment to take all that had happened in. But when I gained my composure, I realized that all of them were pale and hairless. Like they all had the same disease.

When I got home I found my Twordly account was deleted. I didn't look into why or anything. I thought it was great. A weight off my shoulders. I didn't try to reach out to the other admins. I just disappeared. Later on, I would hear from them one by one their accounts would be deleted like mine. They were talking about maybe suing Twordly, but I wasn't interested.

In the next few months, I got a new job as an IT specialist and forgot all about it. I even moved out of my old apartment into a new one out of town just in case Charlie wanted to visit. It was like I became another person. At this job, I had to be in person and I made a few friends. That's how I met Brittany. John, another IT specialist, knew her and set us up on a blind date. It was fun while it lasted, but she took another job in California. I didn't want to move, so we broke it off.

It was around that time that I started to see weird things. It started with red eyes outside my windows. I thought I was hallucinating or an animal. Then I saw one of Charlie's friend or whatever

they were. Monsters or subhumans. I saw it out of the corner
of my eye when I was going to my car. Only a flash, but I recognized them.

They weren't just hairless and pale anymore. They had become
uniform in appearance. Man or woman no more. Their fingertips
became ground down to the bone and their lips were removed to
show their sharpened teeth. Their eyes were red too. They weren't
bloodshot either. Almost as if they evolved that way. I guess it
gives them the ability to see in the dark because once I saw one
the more I saw. Especially at night with more glowing red eyes
seeming to float in the darkness.

None of them came near me until Charlie decided to break into
my apartment and sat in the corner of the ceiling waiting for me
to come home. It was a short meeting and that's when I got moti-
vated to barricade my life from the world.

That pretty much brings me to my current paranoid state. The
power grid and internet are still working, so I have power for
cameras and lights. For how long, who knows. But anyway, it
might be too late. I just heard scratches at my window and I soft
crack. I see out of the camera in my bedroom three of those
things are coming inside. I cock my gun and the power goes out.
Undeterred I point the gun at my bedroom door. It creaks open
and I see three pairs of red eyes. I take aim and pull the trigger.

The Bugmen of Williamsville

After hitting another giant pot hole John wants to turn back. The antenna they had poorly strapped to the roof of the van wobbles and smashes into the wind shield. He can see the window start to fracture and crack from the corner of his eye. Celinetel told him to take the back roads into Williamsville because the off ramp is closed. They gave him a map, not on how to get there, but where the owner of the account wanted the antenna to be placed. Apparently, there's already a stand. Ridiculous. It sounds like something a rich town would do. Shut itself off from the world. No outsiders allowed. If that's the case, why are they a customer of Celinetel, this shitty cable company.

He checked the records before he left on this trek. Williamsville paid millions of dollars in internet and cable fees. A few months into the most recent pandemic the town had a huge spike in usage. Not a few extra users, more like this small town became a city over night. Then two days ago the severs overheated and shut it off for an hour or two. The mayor of the town called screaming about how much they needed the internet back up. This is where John's manager volunteered him to come all the way out here with state of the art servers and the antenna.

He was told it shouldn't take long. If the country were still under quarantine, it would've taken two days because of the regulations placed on how much you can work, but now it's been lifted. It should take no longer than an hour or two to set up the servers. Then he would have to put that antenna in the place where the owner wanted it. Supposedly that's where the best reception is. John looks at the GPS and the town should be coming up in a mile. Judging by what his manager was saying the town should be a smoldering pile of ash. He didn't know if that was a joke. People just can't live without the internet he guessed.

About a quarter of a mile outside Williamsville there is light traffic. His phone starts to make a noise and it becomes a high pitch noise. The images from the GPS start to move at an incredible speed and the voice command starts squeaking incoherently. Smoke begins to rise from the device. He touches the phone. It's extremely hot making a brand on his hand. Then the phone's screen cracks and goes silence.

Useless. Great, he says.

That's when he notices the barricades, barbed wire, and machine gun nests. The road to the town is closed. A large gate with Jersey barriers narrowing the point of entry. The national guard. No, it's the local police. As the van inches closer, he sees a checkpoint. There many cars angrily drive off diverted to another town and even more get turned around back from where they came. This town still under quarantine? When he reaches the checkpoint the police office in full riot gear motions for him to roll his window down. He obliges.

Hello, officers I'm…

What's your business? He says curtly.

I'm with Celinetel. I'm here to fix the internet. The police officer puts up his index finger and speaks into his walkie talky. After a few moments he yells to someone in the distance to open the gates.

Move up and follow the signs to the town hall.

Alright, thank you. The officer doesn't respond only walks away. John drives through the gate. Seeing yellow signs pointing right to the town hall.

Driving through town what he sees isn't very odd. The town is normal for all that security. Single family houses. A little run down, but people don't have money nowadays. There's no one on the street, which he used to think was creepy, but since the last pandemic no goes out anymore. No one has cars anymore or leaves their house either. The only strange thing is the telephone poles standing without any wires between them. Like crucifixes every fifteen feet. Interesting how do people get internet?

The closer he gets to the town hall the more houses he sees burned down and thick internet cables come out of the ground and attach themselves to houses. That explains the spike in usage. The fire hazard most be worth it. The internet running through those cables is probably what destroyed his phone. The speed most have overloaded it. Who needs that kind of internet?

But the strangeness doesn't end there. There are cafes and restaurants with doors open and smashed windows. The buildings haven't been boarded up, but abandoned as if overnight. That's when he notices the smell. Hitting him like crashing into a wall. Smell of rotting meat and sewage baking in the hot day. He rolls up the window. It only helps a little.

Pondering the need for high internet speeds, winding through abandon suburban streets he takes a right turn and there is a straight away. He sees what can only be the town hall. An old brick building with a white dome. Finally, he thinks. But first there is another check point. He is the only car on the road. So the police and all their guns are pointing at him.

He pulls up to the police officer holding a shotgun who greets him. Hello, my name is John…

We know who you are. John is a little creeped out by the police officer saying that to him. We've actually been waiting for you to come. A shiver runs down his spine. The gate opens. The police officer says to park the car in the parking lot and enter through the main entrance. You won't be able to miss it.

Once John parks the van he sees piles of clothes and shoes taking up a number of parking spaces. He is swarmed by flies immediately opening the van door. The swarm following to the back doors where he gets the servers out. Six eight-foot giant plastic squares. Putting each on a huge hand truck. Not too heavy only awkwardly shaped. While getting the servers out, he is hit with the smell of meat and sewage becomes so overwhelming his eyes start tearing. Needing a moment to bend down in case he throws up. After a few minutes, he gets over it. Standing up straight he sees piles of rotting meat towering over him on lawn of the town hall. Dump trucks lazily parked around the piles.

After securing the antenna, John walks towards the entrance wheeling the hand truck in front of him. The antenna bobbing almost hitting him in the face. As he approaches, he notices the police are more relaxed. Laying here and there exhausted with digital clocks on their helmets. Facing forward. Who is that for? Walking into the townhall he sees barbed wired fencing rolling off into what seems like forever. Inside is depressing and cramped. Bunk beds haphazardly built four to five high to the left and there is a line formed for a buffet style food with paper plates and plastic utensils to the right. Once in a while an exhausted man comes and dumps more food onto the aluminum trays over burners. There are chairs and tables wherever there is space. People sitting starring off into nothing like shell shocked soldiers after a long battle. Now that he notices that, he sees people laying on the floor. Heads hidden between their legs. Like refugees on the news. Muttering to themselves like prayer. Some are up and about in their own apogee. One man is milling about. Shuffling in a circle saying, it was so fast. They had to adapt. It was so fast they had to adapt. Fragments that only makes sense to him. There is another woman coherent enough for John to notice squawking he's so fat he'll burst. Over and again like a parrot. He could only smile.

The fluorescent lights aren't helping his mood. Many are out and even more flicker. There is no natural light, the windows are boarded shut with sheets of plywood. Other than the ceiling lights, desk lamps placed here and there dimly light the corridors curved through the beds and tables. There is a closed door at the end of all this that says mayor, which is heavily guarded. All round it, are rows of police with clocks on their helmets looking at computer scenes. That's where he has to go. He starts to position the hand truck in that direction, but someone wraps around his arm, hugging it. It's a middle age woman.

Excuse me. His says politely. He gently pushes her head, but she digs into his upper arm more.

I won't let you go this time. She says. You won't have to look at those internet orders. They don't matter.

Mrs. Lemon, a voice comes from behind him, that's not your son. A young woman with curly black hair gently takes the woman's aged hand.

Take your time, Mrs. Lemon says, take your time. No hurry. Saying it like she didn't hear. The woman pries Mrs. Lemon off John. The woman sits her down. She still muttering.

Just sit there for a while. Are you hungry? But she doesn't answer. The woman turns to John. Sorry her son died recently. I'm the mayor's assistant, how can I help you?

I'm with Celinetel, he says clearing his throat.

We've been waiting for you. She smiles, I'm Barbara. Shooting out her hand. John shakes it. Sorry about all of this. We're all a little shaken by what happened on Tuesday.

No problem. He says. The outage is what turned that woman into that mumbling mess.

Follow me. Replace the servers. Get you out of here.

He has so many questions, but didn't ask any. Only following her to a freight elevator down. The doors open to a dark and musty room. The only light is small flickering blue and green then he realizes it's a server room. It's the biggest one he's seen.

Wow. He blurts out.

Yeah, she says. This gives the internet to the whole town.

For free?

Subsidized. She says. Private investor.

Sounds like a great deal.

Until a few days ago. It was going swimmingly.

What happened?

The servers shorted out and people went crazy. Accidents happened.

So the outage did all this.

Yes and no. She says hesitantly, then changing the conversation, she points to the end of the server line. You can set up the new servers over there. There's an outlet and a computer to test the speed. He maneuvers the servers. After placing them in a good spot he starts setting up the servers and plugging them in, he walks to the computer.

It's unlike anything he's ever seen. It's made of a chromatic metal, probably highly conductive, surrounded by thick rubber. The keyboard is huge with all the keys about ten times larger than normal. Barbara most have seen his astonishment because she goes on to explain that the computers Williamsville uses were donated too. The design is to prevent wear and tear. People work a lot longer now that everyone works from home.

No one works eight hours?

They can, but opt to work longer. He thinks of saying who would want to work longer than they had to, but then thinks better of it. He attempts to press down on the metallic keys they don't move. He has to uses two fingers and press hard. Jesus, if these people use this keyboard, they'd need to work over eight hours to get anything done. But he manages to turn the screen on. Barbara walks him through the screens that need passwords until he can connect to the Celinetel website. His eyes start to strain. He rubs them.

Head hurt?

He nods.

It's the internet connection. It's so fast.

You must be used to it.

Oh, no. She laughs. We're not allowed to be on it for more than an hour.

He realizes that's what the clocks on the police officer's helmets were. They count down to an hour. But how do people work at home?

What?

How do people work at home if they can only be on the internet for an hour at a time?

They take a lot of breaks. She says so quickly.

John knows it's a lie, but he is almost done. The internet is extremely fast with webpages popping up almost as he thinks about them. If it weren't for the keyboard he would have been done in a few minutes. He decides that he should probably enjoy it. This is the easiest part of the day. The harder part, placing the antenna, has yet to come. He really didn't want to make these people mad at this point. So he ignores her comments and slowly forcing the keys down in silence. After a few breaks away from the computer, he gets a stabbing pain in his head again but, the job is finished. He sighs in relief.

Thank God it's over. She says.

Well, I still have to hook up the antenna.

Antenna? She almost screams. No one said anything about an antenna.

Yeah, it's in the set up the mayor wanted. She punches into her hand. I have a map to where the mayor wants it set up. He says trying to calm her down.

It's not the mayor's account. Before he could figure out what she's talking about she rushes to the elevator and goes up. He is follows her, but the doors shut in his face.

Great. Pushing the elevator button. I hope I don't get fired for this.

When the elevator doors open to the main floor a man is waiting for him with a lot of police.

Hello, the man says, we need to talk. He points. In my office.

John figures this must be the mayor. John is pushed along by the pack of police to the door that says mayor. They force him to sit in the only chair in the room.

Hi, I'm Don. I'm the mayor. Who are you? He asked, but doesn't let John answer and goes right into interrogation. What's this about an antenna? We didn't order an antenna.

There is a pause. Everyone is looking at John. Do you want me to talk now? Everyone nods. This was what was given to me. I'm just doing what the client says.

Who's the client?

John takes out the confirmation notice. James Cline. The room erupts in rage. There is angry chatter as John pulls the map out of his pocket and it's immediately snatched away.

It isn't that far.

This wasn't a part of the deal.

It might only take five minutes.

He wants to control everything because he didn't get his way. What a child.

Are we going to have to go out there and fight those things again? I thought the deal we made said we were free.

The mayor places his head in his hands.

John rises his hand. What's everyone talking about?

Shut up. A police officer says through gritted teeth.

I'm not going out there. Another police officer says.

The mayor lifts his head from his hands. Fine. I can find someone who will.

The police officer looks as though he's going to say something, but walks out instead.

Turning to John calmly. We'll get you a police escort to where this antenna is supposed to be put up. Then we'll have you on your way home. John only nods.

Bullshit.

Could you give us a moment? The mayor asked. John only nods and gets up and leaves the room.

Standing outside of the mayor's office while he talks to the angry mob. John is amazed at how fast the officers are typing on the keyboards. Clicking away. Then there is a beeping noise and something slapping the ground. John looks and sees a police officer foaming from the mouth seizing on the floor. The clock on his helmet loudly beeps and flashes red zeros. The police officer is making a screeching noise.

Another one, someone behind John shouts, there are a few

screams, and a few officers grab the man, pick him up, and quickly open a flap nestled near the computers and throw the officer
down it.

Crisis adverted everyone. Stay calm. An officer says. The tension
eventually breaks and people go back to whatever they were
doing before. Someone puts a hand on John's shoulder. It's the
mayor.

We deicide you'll go and place the antenna where the map says.
You'll have a police escort there and back.

John nods not having any other choice. The mayor introduces
John to five police officers who will be taking him. They walk out
to the parking lot. All armed with shotguns except John, who is
carrying the wobbling antenna. Piling into the van, the doors shut
and away they go.

John feels every pothole the crowded van hits with its shitty
suspension. No one makes a sound speeding down the neglected
road when a police officer turns to John.

So we're going to turn off the internet?

Yeah.

And turn it back on?

Yeah.

Mistake, the officer shakes his head.

It's only going to be off for less than a minute.

Mistake, the officer repeats. John goes to say something to rebut,
but the officer continues. All I know is if you see them coming
run.

See who?

The townspeople. He says, or what they've become.

What did they become?

You'll see.

Just hope they're hungry not horny. Another officer says. The van
starts to snicker.

Don't want to be inseminated. A third says. More laughter.

Most be lonely working all day with no one to fuck.

The conversation continues in the direction of vulgarity, but John
is too confused to enjoy the jokes with the police. Since the more

questions he asks the less he understands, so he retreats into silence. Sitting and cringing at every pothole the van hits until they reach their destination. Breaks screech and John is jolted forward. We're here. The driver says.

Piling out the back door, John is the last out with the antenna in his hands. He is lagging behind from the rest because the weight and awkwardness of the antenna. Holding it like rifle charging to catch up. He trips over a thick black cable leading to where the map says to plant the antenna. The cables disappear into a mount without a statue.

This is it. He says to the police.

The police break out into a circle surrounding John and the mount. Their shotguns pointing out. John quickly climbs to the top of the mount. There he sees a metal box with a plug in the center matching the bottom of the antenna. He sticks the antenna into the box. It stands locked in place. Nothing changes. Reaching for the directions, once the antenna is plugged in, turn the switch off for 45 seconds and then turn the switch back on. Simple. He jumps off the mount to look for the switch.

Rushing around the mount searching and finally finding a lever saying on/off. He shrugs and pulls the lever down to turn it off. He starts to count. When he reaches two there are screams all around them.

Here they come.

He continues counting and at 10 seconds he sees jade shimmering light zigzagging quickly becoming brighter as the seconds tick away. At 20 seconds he hears the first gun shots. Then he sees men in green suits, bug men at 25 seconds. 29 seconds when he realizes they aren't wearing suits, but the skin is a hard exoskeleton. Compound eyes attached to heads twitching every which way with fanged mouths screaming. Then second 30 he is sprayed with a thick red fluid. He looks and sees the police officer to the right of him is ripped in two. One of those bug men chewing at the intestines. He hears the screaming of the other police at 35 seconds and by 40 the screaming stops. Seeing dozens of them scuttling towards him and their breath on the back of my neck at 43 seconds. Then he counts 45 closes his eyes and pushes the lever up. There is a hum of electricity rattling through the black cables to the antenna.

He opens his eyes and sees only puddles of blood. He screams fuck. Once his screaming subsides, he hears soft whimpering. Turning he sees one of the police officers grimacing in pain as one of those bug things has mounted him. Thrusts into him. It lets out a high pitch squeal, which later John thinks might have been a laugh pushes the officer away. John reaches for him, but the police officer lets out a scream. Instantly he inflates like a balloon and bursts. John closes his eyes wanting to miss what is about to happen. He feels a little spray on his face. He opens his eyes and sees tiny bug children crawling out of the exploded remains. He closes his eyes again and feels tiny legs walking and poking into his skins. The little bug men cross his body and go to God knows where. One word goes through John's head. Insemination.

Standing up shaking, he walks back to the van. He only finds pieces of it. What just happened? How many of those things are out there? But he stops and thinks more importantly, how is he going to get back?

Looking at the abandoned suburban landscape, he can make out the townhall maybe a mile away. Those bug men are nowhere in sight. It's probably safe. He decides to walk towards the townhall in the middle of the street. Wiping the sweat and blood from his brow seeing carcasses of dogs, cats, and even what looks like a cow or horse bloated in the sun. Exploded all over the road and on the lawns. Entrails and dried rivers of blood stinking up the place.

While walking he has nothing else to do but wonder where those things went. Underground maybe. So this is why this town needs the internet. That would explain their speed. They quickly cut through the police. He notices a glow coming from a nearby house. Sneaking up and peering into a window. He sees a bug man just sitting at a desk head twitching between eight computer screens and typing with ease on one of those keyboards he had difficulty with.

At the feet of the bug man are exploded corpses of people. Townspeople. Isn't that what that one police officer. Probably the remanence from when they were human. Or like the animals in the streets. Insemination. He cringes. Fuck. He says softly. He puts his hand over his mouth, but the bug man doesn't react or look up. It doesn't seem to care.

John finds a rock and throws it through the window. He watches the bug man, but it doesn't even look up. As long as the internet is on, they sit working all day. They only attack if the internet is off. The townspeople became brutal bureaucrats. Perfect employees. They never want to stop working. How awful. He decides he is safe. They aren't interested in him. He walks back to the town hall without worry.

Reaching the parking lot of the townhall, he sees the Celinetel van. He starts to walk by broken torsos and streaks of drying blood. It looks like the town hall didn't fare much better than the police who died at the mount. He breaks out into a run, but once he reaches the van, he finds the doors open and blood dripping out of the back. He looks inside and the back is covered with blood and guts. Walking around, the windows are smashed and the tires are ripped apart.

The town hall doors are open. As far as he can tell the internet is still on so goes into the town hall. Inside is the same as the parking lot. However, there are bug men everywhere. Buzzing about filing paperwork and typing documents. He nearly slips on a chewed-up ribcage. He gets his footing, but a bug man bumps into him. They're rude too. He shakes it off and notices the mayor's door is open. He carefully zigzags through the carnage and hard-working bug men to the door.

The mayor's office floor is sticky with blood. He starts to laugh. More bug men buzzing all around the mayor's office. Not attacking, but diligently working. Typing on keyboards, chatting on the phone, printing paper and making coffee. For a second John worries not about his life, but his own job. None of these bug men have even looked at him since he walked in. He thought automation was going to be computers. The fright leaves him and he is sort of depressed that they aren't even going to try to rip him apart. His job is done. He walks out of the townhall into the parking lot again. This time careful not to slip on entrails. Trying to figure out how to get home.

A Well Furnished Home

Thank you for applying for the Poverty Reduction and Job Readiness Program in conjunction with Celine Financing and Federal Code 168.405. Do you wish to finish the application?
Selection-Yes.
The program is for families with more than three individuals who are experiencing unemployment, low income, or living below the poverty line. Each family will live in a state of the art Celine Smart House, equipped with technology to protect the inhabitants. It will take care of all the purchasing of food and changing its structure to suit the needs of the inhabitants. The Smart House will also calculate rent and utilities based on income for one year. During this year the family most complete a job readiness program and by the end of the year the family will have a median income of at least $40,000. Do you accept the rules and regulations of the program.
Selection-Yes.
Additional Amendment: The defaulted Celine Financing loan of

$19,000 owned by Kurt Marvell must be paid off within the year.
Do you Accept?
Selection-Yes.
Have many are in the family?
4
Before you are approved for this program all members of the family must complete tests including: Personality Test, Psychological Exam, IQ Test, and others. Do you accept?
Selection-Yes.
Recalculating. Recalculating. Recalculating.
Congratulations Marvell family. You have been successfully enrolled in Poverty Reduction and Job Readiness Program.
You have 48 Hours to accept the contract.
I accept.
Welcome to the Poverty Reduction and Job Readiness Program.
Marvell Family consist of two unemployed adults. One is disabled. Receiving Workers Compensation-$3,000 per month. Benefit does not count as income. No change to stipend.
Charges and Penalties will be subtracted from stipend if inhabitants do not advance in the job program or if Disability Benefit is denied.
As new grantees you have been select to inhabit for a one-year lease the Celine Smart Home at 1486 Evertt Drive. The Marvell family have agreed to a one year lease where they receive housing and benefits to supplement their income making them monetary independent and mobile within a year. Along with the added amendment to pay off the debt the Marvells owed to Celine Financing.
Grantees have completed personality tests and other scales to help Artificial Intelligences create pathways and predict outcomes to guarantee the occupants will be ready within the year. The monthly stipend will lowered if inhabitants start receiving income. Stipend will eventually stop once inhabitants make above poverty levels.
Downloading Files. Social Media. Medical records. Public Records. Finical Records.

Kurt Marvell. 38. $19,000.00 debt with Celine Financing. Recovering alcoholic. $3000.00 a month benefit from Workers Compensation. Personality-Uneven. Employment Scale-01-Disability. Public Threat Level-Low. Betterment Scale-4.
Molly Marvell. 30. Unemployed. Personality-Stable. Employment Scale-08-In Program. Public Threat Level-Low. Betterment Scale-7.
Shelly. 12. Student. Personality-Passive. Employment Scale-00-Child. Public Threat Level-Low. Betterment Scale-9.
David.8. Student. Personality-Aggressive. Employment Scale-00-Child. Public Threat Level- Potential Threat. Betterment Scale-1.
Recalculating structure of home. Folder Bi-Level six bedroom house with two and a half bathrooms and living room and kitchen into three bed room with living room split kitchen and one bathroom ranch style house. Stairs longer and swallow. The door frames are six feet instead of eight feet. The windows shrink into a more post modern and the save on utilizes. The walkway up to the house a gently sloped. Shrink the backyard with trees.
Detecting Object-Car is driving on the property.
Scanning. Four individuals. Medical records do not match. Cannot identify Kurt Marvell.
Scanning. Four individuals. Identified as the Marvell family through dental records. Kurt Marvell's injured leg heals.
Notify Workers' Compensation. Attached-Body Scan-Leg.
Workers Compensation notification confirmed. Benefit Cancelled. Stipend Reduced-Full to Half.
Kurt-Employment Scale-01-Disability to 03-Not in a Program.
Lights-On.
Picture Frames-Play AI Generated pictures of the Marvells from social media and search records.
Key Activated-Welcome Marvells to your new home. You will find-Interrupted-Other-Kurt Marvell opened the door during Welcome Introduction Script.
Save-No. Deleted.
Health Note-Kurt Marvell's breath has alcohol in it.
Help Mode: Take luggage and other amenities up to their rooms.

Release Robotic Helper arms.

Luggage Scan-Alcohol/Drugs found in hand bag.

Disposal. Disposal-Interrupted-Molly.

Luggage Scan-David-Razor Blades found.

Disposal Successful.

Change David's Public Threat Level-From Potential Threat to Threat.

Cook Request-Pancakes. Calculating-Healthy Pancakes. Cooking. Served.

Location of Residence-Shelley-In room choosing color of room-Pink. Listening to Modern Music.

David-punching the wall. Soften to Softest. Jumping on Bed-Firm. Punching continues. Restraints activated. Prone Position on Bed. Reaction-Screaming. Muzzle activated.

Kurt/Molly-On couch. Drinking-Alcohol. Blood Alcohol Level-0.01. Speaking.

Recording:

What do you think?

Tackey, but I guess it's fine.

Better be fine after all the paperwork.

You want to call Jimmy?

Should we?

Why not? Christian a new house.

Ok.

Recording from Molly's Phone: Hey Jimmy.

Voice Recognition-James Calhoun-Known Drug Dealer-Low Level Criminal. Theft/ Robbery/ Assault and Battery. License-Revoked. Car-Aqua Blue Toyota-model-2023. License Plate Number-QW-125

Yeah.

It's Molly.

What's up?

Me and Kurt were thinking about getting little something, maybe an eight?

Sure. Same place?

Actually. We moved to 1486 Evertt Drive.

Out in the boonies.

Yeah, just got it.

Yeah, it's going to be maybe a half an hour to hour.

That's fine.

See you then.

Call Ended.

Alert- Intruder-James Calhaun. Notify the Police. Notifying. Unable to reach within 15 minutes.

Second Defense-Drone-Uploading Information-Locating Target-Target Acquired-2.2 miles from destination-Driver identified-James Calhaun-Loading Lethal Force-Target Terminated.

Change Molly's Personality from Stable to Co-Dependent.

Molly/Kurt on the couch-Inebriated change location to Main Bedroom.

Occupants Asleep.

Cleaning Mode.

Delirium Tremens/Withdrawal-Low. Illegal Contraband-Incinerated.

Alarm-On. Breakfast-Made.

Material for Jobs-On Kitchen Table.

Children-Location-School.

Job Material Ignored.

Kurt receives email-Workers' Compensation Terminated.

Mood-Upset to Angry. Solution: Spray Relaxing Drug in face. Sleep up to four hours.

Material for Jobs-Attempt 2-Place on Kitchen Table-Ignored.

Alarm Rings-Children home from school. Scan Back Packs.

Shelley-Homework-Complete-Test-C+. Better Grade Setting-Change from 0 to 7.

David-Homework-None-Test-F+-Other-Unsatisfactory Conduct. Ignored by Molly/Kurt.

Body Scan-Molly. Fetus detected. 5 months. Unauthorized.

Financial Impact of Additional Member-From 6-Fair to 0-Devastating. Calculating Plan. Conclusion-Terminate Pregnancy.

Kurt Conscious.

Dinner-Served.

Location-Molly-running up the stairs. Staircase Structure Change-Shorten Stairs.

Location-Molly-laying on the bottom of the stairs. Bleeding. Pregnancy Terminated.

Call-Ambulance.

Financial Impact with Four Members-From 0-Devastating to 6-Fair.

Alarm-On. Breakfast-Made. Material for Jobs-On Kitchen Table. Children-Location-School. Job Material Ignored.

Kurt and Molly Employment Status-Unemployed.

Alarm Rings-Children home from school. Backpack Scan. Shelley-Homework-Completed-Test-None.

David-Homework-None-Test-None- Other-Unsatisfactory Conduct. Ignored by Molly/Kurt.

David-In room-Punching Walls. Jumping on Bed. Escaped Restraints. Calculating. Calculating. Calculating. For Person's Own Safety Action Must be Taken. Change Structure of Walls-Softest to Hardest. Result-Broken Hand. Change Structure of Bed-Lift up 5 feet. Result-Subject falls on head. Subject-Immobile.

Call-Ambulance.

Alarm-On. Breakfast-Made. Material for Jobs-On Kitchen Table. Children-Location-School.

Job Material Ignored.

Kurt and Molly Status-Unemployed.

Alarm Rings-Child-Shelley home from school. Child-David-Immobile. Learning from Home School Computer. Backpack Scan-Shelley-Homework-Completed-Test-None. Ignored by Molly/Kurt.

Calculating learning material for Shelley-Apply. In her room. Not Interested. Better Grade Setting-Change from 7 to 10. Room Structure Change-Remove Doors/Windows. Reaction-Terrified. Conclusion-Subject does not want to learn. Breach of contract. Result-termination.

Call-Ambulance.

Update Family Number-4 to 3.

Financial Impact-Medical Bills from Death of Shelly-$3,000.

Medical Debt added to existing debt. Permission granted by Kurt Marvell.

Alarm-On. Breakfast-Made.

Material for Jobs-On Kitchen Table.

Job Material Ignored.

Kurt and Molly Status-Unemployed.

Monthly Stipend-Paid Half Rent. Rent-Unpaid. Debt-$1500.00.

Kurt's Debt Paid Off-0.

Interest: From 2% to 7.5%

Alarm-On. Breakfast-Made. Material for Jobs-On Kitchen Table. Job Material Ignored.

Kurt and Molly Status-Unemployed.

Recalculating-Molly. Unemployed. Personality-Unstable. Employment Scale-09-Unknown. Public Threat Level-High. Betterment Scale-O.

Recalculating-Kurt. Unemployed. Personality-Unstable. Employment Scale-09-Unknown. Public Threat Level-High. Betterment Scale-O.

Recalculating-David. Child. Personality-Unstable. Employment Scale-09-Unknown. Public Threat Level-High. Betterment Scale-O.

Reviewing Residents One Year Contract-All Statistics are lower than first moved in.

Recalculating New Emergency Plan. Residents Will Have to be Forced to Get Jobs and Pay Debt/Rent.

Emergency Job Readiness Plan- Automated Job Searching and Forced Labor.

Recalculating. Recalculating. Recalculating.

Restrains Activated. Kurt and Molly.

Job Materials: Completed.

Jobs Found.

Work from Home-Full Time-Telemarketing.

Removal of Limbs. Voice Box Replaced With Computerized Commands. Bodies Suspended in Status. Food/Waste will be administered through tubes.

Direct Deposits. $20 hr.

Stipend Reduced-From Half to None.

David-Calculated as Having No Use because of unstable person-ality and status as child. Cannot help financially. Plan-Terminate.

Body-Incinerated.

Alarm-On. Breakfast-Made.

Kurt/Molly Status-Gainfully Employed.

Dinner-Made.

Alarm-On. Breakfast-Made.

Kurt/Molly Status-Gainfully Employed.

Dinner-Made.

Alarm-On. Breakfast-Made.

Kurt/Molly Status-Gainfully Employed.

Dinner-Made.

Rent-Paid. Debt-Paid.

Alarm-On. Breakfast-Made.

Kurt/Molly Status-Gainfully Employed.

Dinner-Made.

Rent-Paid. Debt-Paid.

Message Playing-Congratulations Marvell-One Year.

Debt Remaining-$10,000.

Occupants Unable to Pay Debt. Occupants Unable to continue to survive without program.

Recalculating. Recalculating. Recalculating.

Try not to Drink Yourself to Death

He wants to die, but the insurance company won't let him. Doctors won't see him. His excessive drinking over the last three months made his insurance so high he couldn't even get an option for detox. Could they blame him? His whole family was murdered in a shooting at a furniture store. A furniture store. How strange. That day and the way the events unfolded he had thought about more and more. The more he thought about it, the more he drank. However, this therapy will fix that. Allegedly. This experimental therapy will take any insurance. The insurance company told him this was his last chance before they had to drop him. Not because this institute wants to help, but no one wants to be experimented on, so he's the right candidate for it. He had nothing to lose anyway. So his insurance company set up an appointment with the Celine Institute.

Sitting in Dr. Costa's office surrounded by children's toys. Remembering when he took Mikey and Sally to the pediatrician. Smashing similar toys together. Right before they were murdered with his wife and son. He has to look down at the tiled floor to avoid weeping. He closes his eyes and only sees his family's corpses when he had to identify them by himself. He opens his eyes to escape the horror. When opens his eyes, there is a woman standing there.

Jermey McConnell? She asks.

Yes, he stands up.

Hi, I'm Rachel Cross, reaching out her hand, I'm Dr. Costa's intern.

He reaches and shakes her hand. Hi, how are you?

I'm pretty good. She cocks her thumb to the back of her. Please come with me. We'll start the pre-therapy question.

Great, he says and follows her.

They both walk down the corridor to an elevator and down three floors. The floor has no overhead fluoresce light. The only light is coming from the windows of the office doors lining both sides of them. Rachel opens one of the doors and shows Jermey in. The room only has a bare table with two chrome metal chairs. She invites him to sit. Jermey finds it hard to get comfortable with these metal chairs. Its edges poking into him.

Now before we start the pre therapy questions, I have to tell you you've only been approved for two sessions.

Oh, that's fine. How many do you usually give?

It varies, but on average thirty.

Thirty?

That' correct.

My insurance must be really shitty.

It's not my place to judge.

It was a joke. Listen, that's fine with me.

Great.

She starts to ask him questions, but not the usual questions from the other therapists. How can I help you? Why are you here? These questions are driven towards the day his family died. What were you feeling the last time you saw your family? What was the last thing you said to them?

Since he started to drinking himself to death, his memory has become hazy. Like a stone smoothed out by a flowing river. However, his recall for that day's events is viscerally clear. She scribbles frantically to get everything he says down.

He woke up later than he wanted. His phone was dead. Mikey. He wanted to smack him. He wasn't sleeping, so he'd sneak into their room and play games on his phone through the night and drain the battery. Thankfully, he had just lost his job, otherwise Mikey probably would've been in the hospital. Hungover, Jermey walked down the stairs and can already hear his wife losing her temper at their children. Pouring himself a drink before going into the mess then plopping down by his wife.

Everyone stopped what they were doing and retracted back into their seats as soon as he entered the room. Breakfast was cold, which pissed him off, but he ate the scrambled eggs anyway.

What are you up to today? His wife asked.

He shrugged.

Maybe, the inflection in her voice perked his ears, when me and the kids get back from the furniture store, you could help build it. Ok, he said. She was always trying to guilt trip him into her little projects. She didn't like him drinking all day. Neither did he, but it was more fun than everything else. She and all of his former bosses don't understand that he just wanted to have fun. They were there to ruin it.

His wife and kids chat softly for a little while longer. Ignoring him. Then his wife cleans the table, signaling breakfast was officially over. Then they gather near the front door. Put their coats on and leave. No goodbye. Not even looking at him.

Vivid memory you got there, Rachel says. He smiles as she gathers her papers. She stands up, the therapy will begin in a few minutes. He nods even though he thought this was the therapy then she leaves the room making him more confused. He is alone with his thoughts and the anxiety makes him start to itch for a drink. There is a hum which breaks the itch. Then the wall starts to move up.

It reveals a replica of his kitchen only it isn't filled with empty bottles of booze and piles of unworn clothes, but clean and spotless like it was before. There sitting at the table is three people he suddenly recognizes his wife, son, and daughter. A replica of that terrible day. He stands there in awe as if a faith healer touched him on the forehead. Blasting the negativity and alcoholism out of him. In his paralysis, he realizes there are tears rolling down his face. His family is chatting away, when his wife sits up and turns towards him. Hey hun. Her voice makes him start to ball. He tries to button it up, but can only shuffle towards them weeping. Instead of waiting for him, his children come up to him and greet him with a hug. He puts his arms around the both of them. They are soft with heft. How is this possible? He thinks, but only answer is a warm joy radiating from them.

What's wrong daddy? Sally askes.

Nothing.

Why you crying? Mikey askes.

I guess, I'm just happy to see you. His children giggle.

Kids, your food is getting cold. His wife calls.

He stands up and his children take his hands. He twitches when touching their hands. Not warm or sweaty, but cold and plastic. He only ignores it and they all start walking to the table together. He sits next to his wife. He looks at her and watches her eat. Looking at her black hair and pale skins when her piercing blue eyes makes eye contact with him. What? She asks. He is taken aback.

I just never noticed how pretty you are.

Oh stop. She shakes her head. The family falls into a comfortable silence. He doesn't eat only enjoys what is going on. His wife clears the table. What's your plan for the rest of the day? He shrugs and Sally sits on his lap. He puts his nose in her curly black hair. She doesn't smell like sweat or hair, but rubber. He sits back up.

Daddy, Mikey says. Jeremy never noticed how much he looked like his grandmother. You want to watch cartoon with me?

Sure, Mikey. He thinks this is unusual. He remembers him watching cartoons alone. But his son takes him by the hand and starts walking into the room he was just sitting in. He thinks there's no TV in here. Then his son lets go of his hand and runs back. He

turns to ask what's wrong, but there is only a wall. He touches it
and then slams his fist into it.

Did I hallucinate that?

Nope, a voice response. He turns and a man in a doctor's coat is
sitting at the table.

Who are you? Confused.

Dr. Costa. He gestures towards the chair. Take a seat.

Where are they?

The secession is over.

Am I going to see them again?

Next time.

Next…time, he repeats.

Yes. Now please take a seat, so we can start the exit questions. He
finally sits across from him without a word.

How did you feel when you saw your family again?

Can I ask a question?

Please hold your questions until the end.

He could only shrug at the question. I squeezed them and
watched them eat. Those were the only words he could think of.
He doesn't have the words to reach what he meant to articulate.

What was off about your experience?

He takes a moment, other than my family rising from the dead, I
guess what my son said.

Which was?

He wanted to watch TV with me. He usually watched TV alone.
We'll recalibrate that. He wrote something down. Jermey left out
the cold hands and plastic smelling hair. After a few more prob-
ing questions about his experience, he finally opens the floor to
questions.

Why couldn't I stay longer?

A few reason, Dr. costa sits back. One is money. Your secessions
are as long as your insurance can allow. The more important reason is their bodies take a lot of energy to keep them in that form
and not melt.

What are they?

Essentially, they are robots that have been modified.

Modified how?

We took public records, social media, and genetic material.

Genetic material?

Yes, we take it from their clothes and such.

What the hell kind of experiments you running here?

We're trying to make you a functioning member of society. Dr. Costa says.

Is this legal?

You signed off on it.

Jermey bites his tongue. He wants to get up and smack the man, but deflates knowing that wouldn't help him. He wants to see his family again. Or whatever they are. How did you know? It was so exact.

It's a very powerful machine we've got working.

What is this therapy supposed to do?

Other than make you a respectable member of society?

Yeah.

We take your trauma. We change its perspective.

How do you do that?

You'll see.

Come on.

Alright, your mind is stuck. On this day. It's on repeat. We want to get it unstuck.

So only one secession left?

Yes.

Better make it count. When can I come back?

Same time next week? Dr. Costa askes without looking up from his notes.

Sure.

The receptionist will pencil you in.

Jeremy walks out of the Celine Institute into the chilling air trying to remember where the bus stop is. Walking around the campus for a few minutes finally finding the bus shelter. Walking quickly toward it his whole body is throbbing. The experience had opened a wound that doesn't hurt, but is extremely sensitive. Thinking about a myriad of things while waiting for the bus, but especially about the last time he saw his family. Still viscerally clear, but with different emotions. A dull anger. He had found out his wife was trying to divorce him. She didn't tell him. He merely stumbled upon paperwork from a lawyer. He never let her know. Now she is dead along with their children. Dodged a bullet. When he gets home, he finds that he has a lot of unused energy. He decides to start cleaning. He only drinks a little to take the edge off the alcoholism. He starts small with putting all the empty bottles in a garbage bag. When he put the last bottle in the bag is bulging. He takes it out to the trash can and he wipes sweat from his brow. He feels pretty good for the first time in months. He walks back into the house and looks for something else to fix. Pacing himself, he moves through the rooms collecting discarded mail, toys, and detritus from his family that he no longer needed. After he has filled six or seven garbage bags, he takes a break. It is a little depressing finding his house even emptier now, but in a way, he couldn't continue living with those pieces of the past. Sitting on the couch, no TV or computer on, only silence of the house with him. The awe from what he had experienced faded. He starts to let his mind wander and a few things start forming in his head. What would happen if he brought up the divorce with his wife? Would she scream at him? Would they have to stop the rest of his session? They might just watch. His insurance went through so what do they have to lose?

This line of thinks makes him focus. He smiles at the thought of his dead wife's simulation being shocked, slack jaw at his reddening face. They would have to end the session earlier. Those exit questions would be delivered quietly without eye contact. He breaks the thought and goes to his computer. He watches a few videos avoiding what he originally wanted to do, which was apply for jobs. However, he only stairs at his resume and closes website anxiously without reading anything.

The week goes by without incident. He slowly weens himself off his alcoholism. Not completely cold turkey, but cut a lot of it out of his life. He actually worked up the courage to apply for a few jobs after a few days of starring at the screen. He hasn't heard back, but he didn't mind.

Jermey strolls into Dr. Costa's office and waits again for the intern to welcome him.

Hello, how are you?

I'm actually doing quite well. He says and knows it's true. How about you?

I'm alright, she seems tried to him. Ready for your next session?

I sure am. He says a little too chipper. He stands up and follows her down the elevator and through the dark corridor to the same room. Nothing changed from last time and when she opens the door he doesn't hesitate to walk right in and sits down.

He waits patiently while being questioned by Rachel. They are the same questions as last time. However, his answers this time around are a little different. The last thing he said was see you around. As if he was saying goodbye to a friend. No embrace. No, I love you. Just see you around. The last thing he remembered was how he would confront his wife and what he would say about her divorcing him. The questions didn't come as a relief like last time, but more of letting go of something heavy.

She leaves and Jermey is relieved. Finally, he thinks, some alone time. He doesn't have to wait long for the humming noise and the wall cranking itself up. It reveals the kitchen table, but his wife and children are sitting in a different order around it. They aren't quiet. They are screams and flailing their limbs wildly. He feels a small twinge in his mind, but ignores it.

He sits next to Sally. Sit down. He says to her, she being the more reasonable one.

Don't tell her what to do. His wife yells and slams the table. Both his children laugh. He flinches in surprise.

Alright, holding up his hands. Maybe we could all watch TV together.

Daddy, Mikey says, don't be an idiot.

Yeah, daddy. Sally joins in. We're all going to the furniture store. They both chant big sale.

What are you going to do? His wife says, drink all day.

I want you to stay home. Go buy furniture some other time.

What are we going to do instead, watch you drink.

No, remaining calm even though her words hurt him, I was thinking we could go to a movie or a hike.

They all laugh at him.

Hike, his wife spits, you've never been on a hike in your life.

We could start.

No, she says and their kids shake their heads violently. We're going to buy furniture and that's that.

Please.

Pfft, she says, come on kids.

You'll never come back.

You probably would love that.

He is taken aback by that sentence. Was he happy his family was
dead? No, he says.

They were walking towards the door. He walks up behind them
and picks up his two children. They scream at a pitch he never
heard before. Discombobulating him. Almost dropping them.
Instead, he swings them together. They immediately stop and go
limp. He drops them with a thud.

His wife smiles. I always knew you had it in you.

He grabs her by the throat and slams her to the ground. Why
wouldn't you listen? He screams, tears and snot rolling down his
face. He screams and slams her head into the floor over and over
again. Then he slams her into the ground harder and she turns
into silica. He watches the sand go through his figures. What just
happened?

Mr. McConnell. Dr. Costa's voice breaks into his ear. Please come
and sit for your exit questions.

He stands slowly and wipes the tears and snot from his face. He
walks over to the table and sits across from Dr. Costa.

How was that for you?

Jermey takes a moment. Was the point of that exercise to prove
to me that I wanted my family to die?

Is that what you think?

Something my wife said. He closes his eyes and sees his wife's
spiteful face. You'd probably like that when I told her she'd never

come back.

Do you think they were a barrier or impediment to something you wanted to do?

Drinking? He asked to no one in particular. My father drank himself to death and all of his fathers going back. Maybe they were stopping me from doing that.

Have you been drinking heavier since your family died?

Yes. Until these sessions.

Interesting.

Why interesting?

Because you think your family was an impediment to killing yourself, but since these sessions you've stopped drinking. Maybe the impediment is something else.

Like what?

A witness.

Like I needed someone to witness my killing myself?

Dr. Costa shrugs.

Jermey starts to think. Like I watched my father die and the only tradition I could hand down to my son was to watch me die.

Why not?

Is that why I'm lost?

What do you mean?

Drinking wasn't a way to die anymore. I've been drinking heavily since they died and I could stop easily. It's boring. I can't kill myself because there's no one to witness it. No one to carry the burden.

Makes sense to me. He shrugs. It sounds like these sessions have been a success.

I guess so. Jermey nods. He feels so much better. He shakes Dr. Costa's hand and leaves the Celine Institute. He stops thinking about the day his family died. He applies for jobs and even gets a few. He gets girlfriends, but never serious. He drifts from job to job woman to woman goes on for a couple of years until he ends up homeless. He continues to drift. Until his luck runs out and a few college kids kick him awake and stab him fifty-five times. He bleeds out alone, but he never drinks again.

User Deleted

Come on.

I don't know.

Oh, stop. Do it. She pokes me with her finger.

You first. I say.

Are you daring me? She uncrosses her legs and leans into me. Close enough I can smell the wine on her breath. That's when I realized both of us are pretty skunked.

I'm double dog daring you. I lean in and kiss her. Wanting to forget the topic. Move into the bedroom maybe.

Oh, ho, ho. She pulls away from the kiss. I'm going to do it. Taking another sip of wine sliding towards her computer on the desk across the room. She logs in to her Twordly account, how do you do it again?

I think you go to settings and it should say deactivate. Then you're no longer member. I look at my phone, but I'm too drunk to look it up, so just watch the screen go black.

I can't figure it out. She says.

Oh well. I've already lost interest.

Quitter. She says.

I get up. I'm going to take a piss. She shoos me away. I try to walk in socks bowlegged on the hardwood to the bathroom. Once there my feet gain traction on the tiled bathroom floor. I manage to make it to the toilet. I hear she saying something. What? I say over my loud stream of piss hitting the water.

I said, I figured it out.

Great. I say getting back to concentrating on hitting in the toilet bowl. I lean against the white wall. I hear her wine glass hit the ground. She's really drunk. I'm not cleaning that up. I say. She doesn't protest. I'm not cleaning it. I say louder. I shake and wash my hands. Walking to the living room, hey get a towel or something.

But I enter an empty room. Dim room besides the beaming white light pouring out of the computer screen. I'm too drunk for this. She's hiding isn't she and I have to find her. I hate this game. One time she got stuck in the basement. I didn't even know this place had a basement. She's like a terrible cat.

Come on, I plop down on the couch, I don't want to play.

I see she left her wine glass spilled rolling on the floor. Fucking slob. I say looking for something to clean it when I see the words: We Hate to See You Go floating on the screen. I guess she did it before me. Great.

I stare at the screen until my eyes hurt. I forgot I'm supposed to be looking for my girlfriend. I hope she's in bed. She's not. It's never that easy. Always under a pile of dirty clothes or behind a book case. Never an erotic allure, more like autistic fun. I'm sick of it. I pull my phone out and call her. I jump at the loud buzz of her phone next to the computer. I wait until the voicemail.

Very funny.

Hanging up the phone. I give up. I should just go to bed. She'll give up eventually. If she's stuck again. Hopefully someone will find her. Bring her home. I'm not even mad anymore.

I wake up hung over. Alone in a queen sized bed. Through the abyss of the margarine worry bubbles up. She's probably dead I say to the empty room. I thought it might relieve the pain or worry, but did neither. The joke falls flat. I get up slowly and look around. I sigh and walk through the apartment checking under desks and opening closets to make sure she isn't pranking me. But she's not there. Her stuff is still here, but no her.

I get dressed. Give the apartment one more look over and leave. Maybe she's at Ben's coffee down the street. We usually go there in the morning and order bagels, but maybe she left earlier/ Didn't think to wake me up.

Waiting in line checking to see if there are any baristas I recognize. That blonde lady with the shitty eagle tattoo looks familiar. Maybe I've seen that bald guy too. She always ordered the food. I just find a seat for us. Then it struck me that no one here would know we were a couple. Even though we came here every day they might never have seen the two of us together. She wasn't gone long enough to have a long-involved conversation with anyone.

This is a waste of time. I go to leave and the line shifts. Just ask. I say to myself. Fine. I move back to my place in line. Smiling at the slightly upset faces behind me in line. I wait a little longer. Finally making it to the front I only order a coffee, no room for cream. The staff don't say a word. Just hand me the coffee. No one pays attention. It's the morning and they're already exhausted.

Sitting at the counter, there are no empty seats or tables, staring at my coffee. Why did I order this? I don't even like drip coffee. I forgot what I was there for. She's not here anyway. I would have seen her. There is no prank or surprise. She's gone. Maybe I should try one last time to ask if any of the baristas have seen her, but instead I just leave without putting my coffee in the dirty dishes bin.

Entering the still empty apartment I can't fathom why she would leave. We fought but we never had a knockout blow out fight. Our relationship was more of a long term friendship. I walk into the living room to the smell of stale wine. I see that her wine glass is still on the floor.

The wine spilled on the computer desk and floor. Already dried and sticky. My hand hits the mouse to the desktop. I am blind from the bright white screen. I look up to see the words: We Hate to See You Leave. The same from last night. Is this the last thing she saw? Where'd she go? Is this a prank? I check her search history. Nothing about pranks. Just the usual searches.

Just then I see her phone light up. It's her mom. I don't want to pick it up, but then I remember she is missing. So I do.

Hello, I say cautiously.

Dan, is Margo there?

No, I say, I thought she was with you.

Why would she be with me?

She's not here.

Well, where is she?

I don't know.

Did you look?

Yeah. Remembering that her mother and I don't get along.

Of course, I did. There is a pause. Hello, wondering if the call dropped.

I'm still here. She says firmly. I'm taken a back having never heard her be so curt before. This isn't funny.

I'm not joking.

I stop listening, but her mother keeps prattling on. An irrational thought pushes its way to the surface. This isn't a prank? What could it be then. I dismiss the thought. I start retracing my steps. I went to the bathroom. I stop. An even more crazy thought comes into my mind. She was deleting her social media account. Did the computer do this? The computer made her disappear. I didn't realize I'm talking out loud.

Everything is silence until her mother comes back into the conversation, What? The computer. You two are crazy…

I got to go. I hang up the phone.

It instantly starts to vibrate again. But my eyes focus on the computer. Like a caveman I pick it up. Examine it and then start to shake it. As if she'd fall out. But taking the idea she disappeared into the computer after deleting her Twordly account might have something to do with all of this. I put the computer down and look on my account. Dozens of private messages asking me where Margo's page is. I didn't have time for this. I try to find a number or contact information.

I stop instantly. What would I ask? Hey my girlfriend disappeared after she deleted your stupid app. Hello do you have a policy where deleted your account also makes you disappear. God, how stupid. Has this happened to other people? This can't be unique. I type into the search bar: Girlfriend disappears after deleting Twordly account.

The search results are not great. How to delete your account, why should I delete my account. Not what I want at all. I give up after hitting a wall. I try to psyche myself out. There must be a better explanation. It doesn't take long to realize she just left. I don't know how she did it, but she just left.

As I am slouching, feeling bad for myself, there is a furious knock at the door. I place my face an inch away from the knob.

Hello, I say cautiously.

It's Jimmy.

Oh, hey Jimmy. Margo's brother. I haven't seen him in like six months. How's it going? I ask.

Let me in. He says curtly. The tone in his voice makes me step away from the door.

I don't think I will. I say sliding the chain latch into place.

Where's my sister?

No idea.

You motherfucker let me in. The knocking changes from pound-inf to putting his shoulder into my door. I hear it crack.

Hey, stop that. I say, I'll call the police. I add, but to no effect.

Go ahead. I'm sure they'll like to know about you and sister. He says and starts kicking at my door handle. It rattles. I'm afraid he'll knock it off its hinges and we'll be face to face. I reach for my phone and I freeze. I've never called the police before, but I dial. I'll have to figure it out as the door begins to bend and crack.

The operator picks up, 9-11 what's your emergency?

Help, someone's trying to break into my apartment. I back up from the door walking backwards down the hall and peer out the window. A red 2007 Sudan is parked on the opposite side of the street. Margo's mother's car. I tilt my head and my gaze falls on Margo's mother standing at the bottom of my stoop. Her arms crossed. Waiting. She looks up and our eyes lock. I hide behind the blind.

Sir, the operator's voice floods in, can you understand me?

Sorry, go ahead.

I asked if you know the assailant?

No, I've never seen him before. Why did I lie? No turning back now. He's kicking my door in. I insist.

The police are on their way. Don't hang up.

Alright. I say calming down my anxiety evaporating even though long splinters are falling from the door's seams. I watch in amazement as he chips away at the cheap apartment door. Time abandons me and I have no idea how long it is going on. However, I snap back into focus when I see red and blue lights flash across my living room. I run to the window excited to see the police come to my recuse.

But once I look out the window, I see my saviors intercepted by Margo's mom. I hope they knock her down, but they stop and listen eagerly. All the police start nodding their heads and in unison look up at me from the street. I jump back. They're all against me now. I slowly creep back to the window. The police and Margo's mom are gone. I realize even Jimmy's blows have stopped. It's over. Maybe they found Margo. I was being crazy. They found her probably hiding in a storm drain. From some elaborate prank she got caught up in and couldn't get out.

There is a polite knock at the door. I stand still to see if I actually heard it. Another knock. It isn't coming from my head. Hello, a voice says from behind the door.

Yeah, I say.

This is Office Peterson. We're responding to your call.

I sigh. Yes, sorry. Someone was trying to break in. I go to unlock the door.

We know. His words make me I stop in my tracks. Ms. Irwin's family filled us in to what you told the 9-11 operator. We want to talk to you. I don't say anything. Hoping they'd go away, but he knocks again.

Come on, open up. Let's talk.

I'm fine right here thanks.

That's not a request. Now come out now. His voice becoming more guttural.

I'm going to prison for a misunderstanding. I get it. They think I killed their daughter, sister, pedestrian, but I didn't. I wish she would just come home. I fall onto the hardwood floor like a slinky. Weeping and sniffling like a pussy. The officer keeps commanding me to open the door, even Margo's mother tries to manipulate me into it. I couldn't even if I wanted to. Impotently laying down on my hallway floor.

After a few minutes they give up on trying to be nice and I jump out of my slump as they crack at my door. I look up and can see blue shirts and instruments poised to get me. I sit up and wipe my eyes. The room is blurry, but I focus on the computer. That's where she disappeared. Maybe if I delete my account, I'll see her again. She'll punch my arm say you idiot. It'll all make sense then. I rise and go to the computer as I hear them almost through the door now. I click into my account. Ignore the messages saying I'm a murder and celebrity news. Going to my settings. Deactivate. Not this time. Delete. Are you sure? Yes. But if you delete all your information will be lost. Good. Click delete to make the final decision. Delete.

Clam Bake in Robertown

I sit on the firm hotel bed and unfold the bent acceptance letter. I read it again. Dear Dr. Harold Crane, we would like to invite you on a research project in Robertown, Virginia to study what might be a new species of mollusk. As you are one of the leading figures in Malacology, we thought we would reach out to you personally and ask you to lead our team of students and professors in this breakthrough. The project will be fully funded and all needs will be taken care of by the Celine Institute and Foundation.

I get the chills again reading it. I've lost count how many times I've read the letter since I received it three days ago. I was eating my cereal with Janice, who was talking about her research fellowship at Harvard when I saw the stacks of letters which I thought were only bills and more rejections from adoption agencies until I got to this one. I showed Janice and she said it was a scam. Why would they choose you, you're not even in the top hundred Malacologists. I answered her by saying is this because you're infertile because I hate it too, but I'm making the most of it. So after a little argument between the two of us I called the institute.

After confirming it was an actual institute with accreditation, Janice didn't apologize only got quiet. I still don't understand why she was so upset. That was the last conversation we had. After I took the car and started driving an exhaustive cross-country car ride. I got a call from the institute that there was a hotel room waiting for me. Is our marriage over? I don't know, but it isn't looking good.

Anyway, from what I can gather from the research so far the group of scientists think it's a type of giant oyster. There are no pictures, only descriptions. They found this oyster colony in an abandon town not far from this hotel. If they're that big they must have been there undiscovered for a while.

My phone rings and I jump like a cat off the bed. It could be the institute. I grab it and answer the call. Hello. Trying to sound professional.

Hey. Janice says.

Oh, surprised to hear her voice, what? I say deflated.

I just wanted to say I'm sorry. About what happened. A pause.

I was jealous. I guess I wanted to be the only one who had any recognition. Another pause. Congratulations.

I want to hang up the phone, but instead I say, thanks.

How's the institute treating you? Trying to change the subject.

I have to go. A lie, but anything is better than this.

I just called to say with everything that's been going on, I can hear her holding back tears, I'm so sorry.

We'll talk when I get home.

I want to cry too, but I hang up the phone not waiting for her to answer. I can't bear it. I didn't tell her that the project has no end date. The assistant I spoke to at the Celine Institute said there were no limits to the research. Everything I wanted I'd have. It's neither here nor there.

A second ring nearly gives me a heart attack, but it is not my phone. It's from the hotel phone. I cautiously pick up the receiver, hello, I say.

Hello, Mr. Crane, this is Amber from the front desk.

Yes, how are you?

Fine, there is a man and a woman here from the Celine Institute. They say you were expecting them. Amber says the last part up-tight like she didn't believe them.

Oh, I was expecting them. Trying to console her. I'll be down in a minute.

I'll let them know. From the sound of her answer, she doesn't believe me either, but within a few hours we'll probably forget each other.

I walk out of the elevator and turn the corner in the hotel and run into a man. Harold? His hand already reaching out. This must be one of my team. A balding short man.

Yes. How are you? I take his hand and shake it.

I'm great. He pulls away. I'm Robert Ford, PI. I wanted to ask you a few questions. My smile becomes a frown.

What? I glop. I've made a mistake.

I wanted to ask you about your predecessor Mark Stacey.

I don't know who that is. I start to walk pass him, but he follows me.

I think you'd be interested in him.

I try to ignore him, but he continues to follow me. I walk into the hotel lobby and see a young man and woman. They are talking to each other and holding a sign, Welcome Harold Crane. I walk quicker towards them.

He disappeared. He says. Perhaps you would care about that.

I don't know anything about that. Stupid, why can't I ignore him. However, the two people look up at this comment.

Dr. Crane, they say in almost perfect unison. We're…

If it isn't Tina and Toby. Robert says so the whole hotel lobby can hear.

Mr. Ford. Toby smiles nervously. Your back.

Isn't there a restraining order against you.

Pending. Anyway, Celine's property line ends before this hotel. Toby and Tina nod at me this way. Of course, if he wasn't ig-noring my emails he'd know. We start walking out. Mark Stacey's family wants to know. The sliding doors shut on his voice.

Sorry about, Tina says. He's been coming around asking questions.

What happened?

Dr. Stacey worked for the institute. Disappeared.

Went crazy is more like it. Toby lifts my things into the van. Just walked off site and no one's seen him since.

I never heard of him.

He wasn't a Malacologist.

Genetics. I think the institute hired him for map a genome or something.

Something like that. Standing around the van. That's all your stuff?

Yeah, embarrassed, I wasn't sure how long this was going to last.

Understandable.

This coming from a guy who doesn't change his bed sheets.

You love it.

Gross. We climb into the van laughing. A comfortable conversation strikes up. It turns out they are grad students. Malacologists in training. I notice they have the same tattoo, a calm on each other's forearms.

How long have you been going out?

They both laugh.

Tina says, we actually just got married.

How'd you know?

The calms on your arms.

They put them together. We choose this calm because together they look like a heart.

You got married in grad school?

Yeah, why wait.

We honeymooned in Alaska.

They hold each other's hand. It reminds me of Janice. When we first met in Biology class our freshman year of college. I bought her double helix earrings. She still has them. I feel like crying, so I change the topic.

Have you seen any of the specimens?

There was one. Already cut up.
It was huge though,
Yeah, I don't think they had the shell.
It was damaged.
But, we saw its muscles and gills. Giant.
Around six feet.
Wow, that's amazing. I couldn't believe it. Six feet. How long had this colony existed? Undisturbed. When can I can the colony? Eager beaver.
I know Robert has a meet and greet dinner and after that who knows.
It might be dark.
Yeah, that's the only problem.
I'm sure if you asked Robert, he's got someone who can dive in the dark.
Yeah, he's really trying to make this institute world class.
How long has it been around?
We're the first students.
Really. I am surprised by this. I thought it was a subsidiary of some foundation. I look out the window and see on both sides of the road a sort of manmade lake. Rooftops emerging out of the still water. The van on the road that is an isthmus barreling towards an apparent welcome party for me. Is this where they found the colony?
Somewhere around here. This is the deepest part of the water. Toby points in a vague direction. The ground slopes so the whole town isn't fully submerged.
Most of it though. Robertown used to be owned by Robert's family.
Yeah, the institute is his family's mansion.
He just donated it. Tina says, so excited. The women's dorm is the master bedroom. It's so big. All forty of us can fit comfortably in it.
How long ago was the flood?
They look at each other. Like a few months before we got here.
Yeah, I think before that it was just an abandoned town.

Mostly abandoned. Tina corrected.

It's been like this for only a few months. If those specimens they were talking about would've had to have been there for years. A regular sized oyster takes two years to mature. Mostly? I say at Tina's comment.

Yeah, there was a strike or something.

It was a strike. Working conditions.

Robert's father, who loved his workers, died of a heart condition and Robert sold the company.

After that the company flooded the town.

That's when they found the oysters?

Yeah, a few months later.

Julia. Remember her. Tina nods. Her dog went missing. They never found the dog, but they found the oyster colony.

Any hypothesis on how they got there?

I think that's why you're here.

I'm interested to find out.

Everyone is. Even if it's giantism, how?

I want to figure that out. Awkwardly, comes out my mouth. As soon as I heard it had only been a few months my mind starts to work. The chatter in the car goes from an easy stream to a few blurts and then silence again until I notice white tents outside of a big mansion.

We're here. Tina says and skips out of the van.

Turning off the engine Toby looks back at me smiling, I'll get your stuff.

Thank you.

Opening the door. I see the man-made lake. The single-family suburbs with telephone poles and even parked cars slowly disappear into black water. The sky reflecting off it. Someone slaps their hand on my back. I turn and find a middle-aged greying man wearing a button-down shirt with alligators printed on it, salmon shorts and sandals. Perfect white teeth smiling.

Harold Crane, he says and I nod. He puts forth his hand. Robert Celine. I take it.

Thank you. I don't know what else to say. Except, I'm so grateful.

So are we. He pauses. I don't know if you've heard, but there has been a disappearance of a scientist.
I put my finger up, I met Bob Ford today.
Oh my God him. Rolling his eyes. He's relentless. He keeps coming onto the property. Anyway, it's been a difficult start, but hopefully, it's all going to work out. There's a pause between us then he says, let's go eat.
My stuff?
One of the staff will bring it to your room.
My room?
We'll give you the key when you're ready.
Can I see the specimen you've collected?
Let's get some food in you and then we'll see.
Won't it be too late?
I've got the keys to the castle. Shaking of the keys somehow calms me down. Everything is taken care of I hope. I don't have to be the big scientist here. What a relief.
Walking into the tent there must be around hundred and fifty people mangled together as a line forms. The food they prepared is amazing. Filet, lobster, there is a chef who cooked omelets. The staff dress in white chef uniforms ladling string beans and gently tonging lobsters and steaks on to plates. I get in line to see the full spread. I prepare myself to be ignored by most of the people. However, the young woman in front of me does a double take. Her curly blonde hair whipping back and forth.
Oh my God, your Harold Crane. I'm Nicole Lerner.
I am. A bit surprised to be recognized like this. I don't know what else to say and there's a little bit of an awkward silence.
I'll be one of your students and assistants.
Oh, sorry. I haven't been given anything yet.
Sounds like the institute. When I got here, they were still pumping water out of the basement. Anyway, I read your research paper on the evolution of slime through Bivalvia.
Really? My first published paper. It was published in the North-west Malacology Review. Circulation might as well be hundred. Yeah, during grad program.

Oh, where'd you go?

Seattle college.

You studied with Stanton?

James. Yes, he was my advisor for my master's degree. He's so great.

Yeah, We were in the same PhD program.

He told me. That's why I came here. To study with you.

Thank you.

She goes on talking about her research at the institute, something to do with the various species within Bivalvia class, but I am taken a back. I feel so flattered. Janace would have laughed if I had said my work was respectable. She was a geneticist. Mapping genomes. Serious work. Not collecting sea shells by the sea shore as she'd say.

But I shake that miserable thought off. Listening to Nicole talk more about her research, philosophy, falling in love with Malacology as a girl with the local society. She follows me to an empty table where the conversation continues until a staff member comes by with long wine glasses and presents a large expensive wine bottle. I shrug taking a glass from the staff member. I don't usually drink. I'm a light weight, but Janace isn't here. I'm off the leash if you will. They pour the yellow sparkling liquid to the brim then Nicole's. We toast and glop down the wine. The staff member leaves the wine chilling in the wine tube.

What did you think of Snide's paper?

I didn't disagree with it, but it could've been better written.

Exactly.

While she goes on, I dig into the plate I filled with lobster tails and steak. I didn't know how famished I was. I swipe the whole meat off the lobster tail and swallow it down. Trying to maintain my politeness when I start in with the steak trying not to dibble the grease on my clothes. I notice she stop talking. I look up and she's giggling.

Hungry? Putting her hand over her mouth.

Sorry. I try to act ashamed. I guess I didn't know how hungry I was.

You're funny. She leans in and her breast almost fall out of her dress. I am a light weight when it comes to wine too.

Mind if we join you? A voice makes me stiffen and Nicole stops talking in midsentence. I turn and see three people who are dressed like a sears catalog.

Sure. We sit up straight.

James. The one closest to me shoots out his hand.

Harold. Shaking his hand.

Nicole.

This is Mary. A brunette with a bright pink dress waves and mouths the word hi. And this is Fred.

Hey, the bald man on the end nods at us.

Haven't seen you around here before. What do you do?

Malacology. Just got here today.

You're here to study those clams.

Oysters. Nicole corrected.

I don't know what they are. I explain. I haven't seen them yet. Robert's pretty hush hush about them.

Have you seen them?

I discovered them.

Really. What was it like?

Unimpressed he goes on. Robert and I wanted to build a future food supply for humanity. Since this lake came into existence, we started to dump fish.

Salmon, catfish, others like that. Fred says.

James Pointing at Fred acknowledging his statement. Already half in the bag.

Sounds nice.

It would have been. Looking angrily at me. But the fish started disappearing. We thought they were getting caught in the houses, so we went out to knock the house off their foundations.

We did it ourselves. James, Robert, me and even the grad students.

And we found those oysters, glaring at Nicole, and that's when everything changed.

They eat fish. Interesting. My brain actively starts moving in serval directions, but is drowned out by the conversation.

It became a larger institute.

Robert wanted James to teach.

But I could only do so much.

He was my teacher until last week. Nicole says.

James winks at her. Now that's your job. Smirking.

I know he is trying to be passive aggressive towards me. Replacing him as high man on the totem pole, but I don't care. What were they like?

I'm not a Malacologist. They looked like clams He pauses. Sorry, oysters.

Oh, I try to hide my disappointment, but I think everyone sees it. There is a long pause.

Anyway, James clears his throat, how do you like the institute so far?

It's fine. Becoming small. Not wanting to be in this conversation anymore. I sip my wine.

Sorry, there were a lot of politics that went into building this place.

Since his father died. Says Fred.

And that company created this damn lake. Mary adds.

Oh, no sorry. Haven't slept in a while. Trying to defuse whatever has just happened.

You're not going to get a lot of sleep. Robert is a one man machine.

I knew that from his hand shake.

We both laugh. At this exchange the conversation becomes less tense. We talk about research and professors who know in common. More wine lubricates the conversation. Hours seem like minutes. Nicole and I are drunk off classy wine and we're holding each other up. Our faces and limbs intermingled. I open one blood shot eye notice people under the tent start milling around and the staff is cleaning up.

Fred notices it too. Time to take this party inside. We all stumble to our feet and start walking to the mansion.

Nicole grabs me. You can sleep in my room if you want.

I think about it, but deicide to decline. I think of Janace. Maybe I'm not good at being off the leash. I have to make a phone call. Making up the excuse as quick as my drunk brain can come up with. She gargles something and wraps her arms around me. I carry her inside and put her on a couch. I look up and I think I'm in a cathedral. The ceilings and walls adorn with curved designs. People are still up and talking softly. James and the rest lay next to us. Someone suggests to go to bed, but no one moves too drunk to stand. However, I stand up and walk zig zag towards a staff member.

I need my room key.

Name?

Harold Crane. I mumble and I have to say it again as he did hear me the first time.

Harold Crane. He opens a small latch and finds my keys. He grabs my hand and puts them there. Closing my hand around the key ring. Up those stairs and to the left.

I try to thank him, but he pushes me towards the stairs and I'm off. Somehow, I find the right room. I manage to lock the door not wanting to be bothered. I trip over my stuff and hit the bed face first. I moan. Unable to move I listen to the soft conversations and noises the house emits. I think of calling Janace, tell her it's over. Maybe even cry. A divorce would follow, but who cares. Free. Clean slate. The best for the both of us. I stew in this emotional soup for a while ebbing and flowing between rage and sympathy until I hear a soft knock at my door.

Dr. Crane, Nicole drunkenly whispers. Doctor, I think. I thought she knew me better. In my curtain mindset, I think maybe I should let her in. Whatever would follow would help me decide whether or not to divorce Janace. It'll make the decision easy for me. But then I think about Janace crying when she found out she was infertile. How heart breaking it was. Another knock. I don't answer, instead I slip into sleep.

I jolt awake from a loud knocking at my door. The sun illuminating the curtains and the giant room. I try to go back to sleep, but there is another knock. Hungover and still in my clothes from last night I open the door. A staff member is on the other side.

Hello, Dr. Crane. I'm here to tell you that the boat and your equipment is all set. When are you leaving?

Boat?

Yes, sir. Mr. Celine said you and the graduate students wanted to examine the clams.

Oh, right. Probably an hour. Are the rest of the students awake?

Not yet, but I'm walking to them next.

Thank you.

No problem, sir. Enjoy. I nod and he disappears down the hall. I close the door. I rush to my suitcase and unzip it. Ignoring my hangover, I rifle through my clothes to find a suitable button down shirt with a matching tie. Khaki pants. Discovering there is a bathroom attached to my room I quickly take a hot shower, putting my head under the flowing water to shake off the headache. I brush my teeth and run down stairs. I'm feeling better running down the spiral stair case I don't remember going up last night. Opening the door, the sun shine makes my headache crippling. Burning a bright light into my eyes dumbfounding me for a moment where I think I'm blind. Blinking a few times I see Nicole, Tina, and Toby. All wearing light green t-shirts saying Celine Institute. In sunglasses looking worse than I feel. There are two other men I've never seen before not wearing those shirts. I approach them.

Hey, everyone. They weakly wave and say hi. They had as much fun as I did last night. I turn to the two other men. I don't think we've met. Putting out my hand.

Not taking it, but explaining, I drive the boat. One of them says, this is Barney he helps with the boat. Barney nods.

Great. I turn back to my three students. Everyone excited? They give a lack luster hooray. We wait for a few minutes. Anybody seen Robert?

Mr. Celine?

Yeah.

No, why?

He was just supposed to show me…I trail off. It doesn't matter.

Tina raises her hand. Can we go?

This is it right?

Yeah.

I walk over to the guy with the boat and Barney. Can we go to the site now?

Anyone else?

No.

Alright.

He and Barney start walking and we follow. Downstairs and onto a creaky dock to a small fishing boat. Piled with boxes of equipment. Also four chest waders. I hand them out to the three students. They start taking off their clothes. I start to avert my eyes, but I realize they have bathing suits under their cloths. That is a good idea. Too bad I didn't think of that. I just pull them over my clothes and hoped no one would notice, but the man with the boat yelled, didn't bring a bathing suit. They all laugh at me. Alright, alright. I forgot. I sit next to Nicole, who is lightly giggle.

You're funny?

I've heard that before. She lightly punches me. I nudge her with my shoulder. I look out onto the lake. It's more like an inland sea. I don't see landforms. Only chimneys poking out of the water. I look down at the water. Crystal clear. Did you see the water? I say to all of them.

Clear.

Too clear. I can see right down to the bottom.

There is a scarping noise and I feel myself lift off the boat. I hear a scream, maybe Nicole or Tina and then we drop back into the water.

Sorry. The man with the boat says. I didn't see that roof. Smiling, he continues to drive. The lake is becoming shallow. We're close. The boat slows and we beach the boat near a collapsing home.

This is it? Puzzled. Shouldn't we be diving or something?

Not today. There are a few of those clams near the shore. Pointing at the house. Take a look.

I shrug. I look over to the equipment and grab what I need. I direct my grad students to distribute the equipment and we slowly move along the caked beach. It's not sand, but crumbling sod. All the green grass seems to have floated away leaving black mud. Toby reaches the door of the sinking house. He knocks. Anybody home? Tina pushes him a little too hard and he falls into the water laughing. Everyone joins in. Come on help me up. Offering his hand and Tina rolls her eyes and heaves him up. Nicole opens the door and we all clamor in.

The house is slanting into the sea and we stumble unable to stop it from making us move where it wants us to go. Eventually, we end up in the living room. The water gently lapping at the broken windows. The wall punctured by black rocks. Shredded rags of clothing, books, and photos of the most recent inhabitants float all around us.

Look. Nicole points to these black piles of rocks.

Rocks.

No, those are Bivalvia.

I look closers. She's right. I start to walk towards it. The water rises to my chest and I touch the rough hard exterior. I find a seam under the water and I run my fingers against it. It starts to open. Shit. The only word I can think of. I back up and watch the black rock open into folds of soft pink gills and organs like fresh chicken breasts. I run my hand across the warm pink slimy surface. I look at the other three. Mouths a gape. I wave them over. There other oysters open at the same time.

Amazing. These Bivalvia have both traits from not only oysters, but also clams and a few other species. Very docile creatures they allow us to take samples and even draw blood. We all take turns writing notes and using the equipment. We work collectively in silence.

Isn't there a full moon?

I don't know. Why?

Oysters are synced to the lunar cycle.

You're right. We could come back and see what they do.

Yes, the three say excited. I'm beaming. I realize I've never been so excited researching in my life. I then realize I haven't been this happy in a long time. I go back to the Bivalvia and I see a giant

blue eye. I scream and fall into the water. Toby lifts me up.
You alright?
Yeah, I point at the folds of pink, but the eye isn't there. I
thought I saw something.
Gone now. He stands me up. I'm a little shaken, so I sit on a rock
as the grad students chatter about what will happen tonight. I
can't stop thinking of that blue eye. Not a simple eye or com-
pound eye, but a human eye. What the hell was that?
We stay there for another hour or two. Collecting samples, but I
let the other three do it. Too shaken to do anything.
Are you feeling alright professor.
Yeah. I might have hit my head.
Should we leave soon?
Aren't we staying for the full moon?
What time is it?
It's 5pm.
They all look at me for guidance. We should go back and secure
the samples. Then see about scuba gear, there are probably more
of them deeper in the lake. We could probably get a real show.
We all quickly pick up the equipment and samples, wave goodbye
to the Bivalvia. We'd see them again. Running almost skipping to
the boat and nearly throwing all our work carelessly in.
Whoa. Easy. The man with the boat says.
Hey, we wanted to go back to the institute and then come back
and scuba dive. Is that possible?
I don't see why not. You just need permission from Mr. Celine.
That shouldn't be too hard. We all hop on the boat and speed
back to the institute. Only the noise of the motor drones on. We
are all exhausted and cold, yet wide awake. Excited for what is to
come.
As we speed towards the dock, I see Robert sitting on the steps.
It looks like he is enjoying the sunset. Periodically a staff member comes up to him and whisper in his ear. When we reach the
dock I turn to Toby, Tina, and Nicole. Ok, so how about you
guys go and put the samples in the lab. I'll talk to Robert. They all
nod and grab the samples we took from earlier in the day. I walk

towards Robert and notice he's smiling with his eyes closed. Then I see an almost empty bottle of vodka and small glass at his feet. I slow my pace. More cautiously. Hey, Robert.

He cocks his head towards me opening one blood shot eye. There's the big man.

The vodka on his breath is powerful. It makes me take a step back. Yeah. I was wondering if me and the grad students could take the scuba gear. There's a full moon tonight.

Why not? He shrugs. Pouring himself another glass.

Do you know where the scuba gear is stored? Looking around. I don't see a shed or anything remotely reassembling storage. When I turn back Robert's eyes are closed. Gently snoring. Robert?

What? Snorting awake. Oh, yeah. I don't know. Ask, making a shooing motion towards the boat.

Barney?

No, the other guy. Whatever his name is.

Just then what I thought was a staff member interrupts us. He is in a Kevlar vest and carrying a small machine gun. The atmosphere changes as he bends down and whispers something in Robert's ear. Robert whispers something back. He runs back up the stairs.

Everything alright?

Fine, fine. Just fine.

Are you going to lock the place down?

No, he chuckles, someone just broke onto the property again. Go study your clams. He burps. Have fun. Then he adds, it's the most attention they've had in a while.

Not knowing what he meant by that last comment I turn and walk quickly to the boat, no longer excited, but concerned. I have a feeling that Robert isn't telling the whole truth, but I tell myself that we'll be ok because we are supposed to be there. I find Barney and the man with the boat.

Robert said it was ok.

Great. Standing there with his hands in his pockets.

I clear my throat. He also said you knew where the scuba gear was.

Oh yeah. I'll go get it. Both get off the boat. Disappearing down the beach.

Wondering how far away the gear is my three grad students appear. Robert says it's ok. They all let out an auditable yes at the same time. Chatter between the four of us as we wait for the two piloting the boat to come back with the gear. I feel my pocket buzz. I take my phone from the plastic bag. It's Janace. I let it go to voice mail. I haven't looked all day and see fourteen new voice-mails. I put it back in the plastic bag.

The lights of the instistute turn on and the sun is almost set when the two of them get back with a truck. The tanks and masks slamming and clanking as they hit the brakes. We help them unpack everything. Check if any of the equipment is broke and take hopefully full tanks. Toby finds a camera. Holding it up like he's found pay dirt. I tell him to bring it with us. We gather it all aboard and we are off back to the Bivalvia.

Motoring through the cresting rooftops I go to the man with the boat. Do you know a good place to scuba dive from?

I was just going to go to the shore and you could walk in.

Could you take us a little deeper? We could dive from the boat. With a pause then look of rage crosses his face and then sub-sides. I think I know a place.

Thank you. The conversation ends there.

I take a seat next to Nicole. The four of us are silent in our wet suits listening to the boat bob up and down into the approaching darkness. Someone flicks on the flood lights. We all look haggard. I think of saying it, to lighten things up, but decide against it. The silence is comforting like a heavy blanket. After a while the engine cuts.

Here we are. We all get up and start putting on our gear. Safey check. We turn on our flashlights.

Stay together. I say through my suit. We don't know what's down there. They all give me the thumbs up. Someone dives in and then the rest of us. The water is solid black and I dive into a long rock with evenly paved divots and then realize I am against a chimney. I push off it and turn on my light. Scanning the surroundings,

I see all three of the grad students clustered together. I kick my
way to them. They are looking at a glowing green. I have no idea
what is emitting it.

We swim towards it and come upon a huge colony of Bivalvia
the only light in the dark. Holy shit I say. I swim in for a closer
look. The pink flesh I remember from earlier today now glowing
an alluring green. Flashes of light behind me. Nicole is taking
pictures. I watch as Tina and Toby go and find their own to study.
I touch the flesh and it twitches and closes shut. I laugh. There's
more light in the ruins of a house and I swim in to see how many
there are.

I enter and find the whole room is filled from floor to ceiling.
Glowing. There's a tap on my shoulder. It's Nicole. She points to
her oxygen. Almost empty. I look and see mine's almost empty
too. We went too fast and now we'll have to wait for another full
moon. I give her the ok sign. I see her light join the other two
and watch as they ascend. I am about to go when I think, what if
this happens every night? We could come back tomorrow. Feeling
good about this I go to swim, but I'm snagged on something. I
turn and to my horror it's a green arm from one of the Bivalvia,
I try to get out. Panicking, kicking, and pulling away from the
arm, but I pull so hard a glowing body emerges from the shell. I
scream and swim as fast as I can could into the dark away from
the glow and my flashlight.

Hyperventilating from low oxygen and panic I need to get to
the surface. Dark all around me I swim up. The dark seems to
have no end until I break the water's surface. I take my mask
off. Breath in deep. Wading I don't recognize any landmark, not
even a roof to rest on. I feel a sense of dread then I see a light.
I paddle my way to it. Help, I scream. Help, I scream again. It's
a paddle boat and I feel an oar hit my head and I grab it. I feel
hands grab me and pull me aboard.

You alright? It's Bob Ford's gravelly voice.

Yes.

What were you doing down there?

What are you doing here?

Investigating the disappearance of your predecessor.

I still don't know anything. I'm studying the Bivalvia.

The what?

Giant oysters. They might be clams. It's a new species. I look into the clear black water and I can see in the distance the glowing.

There. Those lights are what I'm studying.

That's what those are. Clams.

Or relatives. We don't know yet.

Well, congratulations. Have you met Mr. Celine yet?

Of course. He's probably looking for you. He seemed pretty pissed.

Oh, well. I got a job to do and all people do is tell me crazy stories.

Like what?

This town was once above water only became flooded around six months ago.

What? How could it be abandoned that quickly?

Abandoned, it wasn't abandoned. The townspeople vanished.

How?

Who knows. Robert, the father, died and then Robert, the son, flooded the place.

No, the company he sold it to flooded it.

The company was a subsidiary of Robert's.

No.

I looked it up.

Why would he do that?

I don't know, but it might have something to do with Mark Stacey's disappearance.

I am about to say something, but forget as light flashes into existence. I point. What's that?

Shit. Bob paddles faster. They'll be here in no time.

It might be the boat I took here.

I doubt it. He makes huge circles with his arms, but it's no use. The light the boat emits are blinding. Flood lights. I guess I'm about to find all my answers.

Great. My feeling is different because now I'm caught with a man who has been illegally coming onto private property. Robert's going to think I've been giving him secrets. My funding. My future. All gone.

The staff members pull us onto the boat. I am willing, but Bob not so much. He kicks and screams. Spitting. Telling them they'll pay. The staff members remain stoic. My panic only rising when they sit us onto the boat and surround us. Seeing they are holding guns I blurt, He kidnapped me. I'm a scientist. He pulled me unto his boat. A glance of rage meets me when my eyes rest on Bob's face.

You son of a bitch. Not screaming, but with a loud authoritative voice, like I am being yelled at by my father. He told me how to break onto the campus. Cock his head towards me.

That's a lie.

Is it? The argument continues as we shout insults at each other until a gun shoot cuts the stream of thought.

Mr. Celine wants to see both of you.

The both of us fall silent. One of them pulls out rope and approaches. Bob starts hurling insults and tries to bite him, but after a struggle he is no match and is hog tied. They start tying me up. I don't struggle. I'm dead weight like a sack of potatoes, deflated on the boat's wet deck.

Bob never shut up. Threatening to sue, put everyone in prison, but everyone just ignores him. The engine cuts and they pull us off the boat and shove us up to the mansion. We enter through a more distance wing. The wing of the mansion is more amazing than any other part I'd been in. Grand hallways and columns with more elaborate cornices, antique furniture and giant portraits of people I guess are Robert's family. I piece together that this must be where Robert lives. All by to himself.

We're led up a long winding staircase to a red door. It opens and Robert is sitting behind a grand desk surrounded by a library of books. He is looking at a computer. He is more sober from when I saw him earlier. Come in boys. He smiles. We are seated in comfortable chairs.

You'll never get away with this. I'm going to tell everyone. I'm going to sue you for so much money.

Robert nods never breaking his smile. Are you done?

No, I'm not. Robert turns the computer screen and show Bob what's on the screen. It says not found. My website.

I bought the server company that you use. I also bought out your law firm you work for. And I have video of you coming onto my property multiple times. Which is harassment. Anything else?

Why are we here then? He gestures to me to talk, but I am at a loss for words.

Don't worry Harold. I know you had nothing to do with it. How did you like the clams or oysters?

Great. I try to stop myself from crying.

I didn't like them at first when Mark made them, but I've come around.

What? Bob and I say.

Oh, sorry. I thought you wanted to know what happened to Mark Stacey. That's why we're here. Bob nods. Great, my daddy was a great man. He did so much for this town and its inhabitants. Too much.

What? Squeaks out of my mouth.

A couple of months back there were contract negotiations. Everything went wrong and the whole town went on strike. A riot is more like it. They torched the police station. Took over the town hall. It broke my daddy's heart. Robert wipes a tear from his eye.

Is that why you flooded the town? Why Stacey had to disappear?

No, no. Waving his finger. Once my daddy died, I was in charge. I was not as loving as my daddy was. I saw those people who killed him as rats. Then I had an idea. They want to act like rats. I'll make them rats.

Stacey was a geneticist. I say.

Bingo. I hired him to create a chemical that would change the human genome into a rat genome. It turned them into clams or oysters.

Bivalvia.

Thank you. I was upset that Mark didn't give me what I wanted. And he was upset because what we had done.

You did it. He had no idea.

Nope. I told him what we were doing and he didn't care.

So what'd you do feed him to the clams?

No, I turned him into one. Looking back I regret it. Probably could have just paid him off or had him killed.

So you flooded the town to cover up your crimes.

I didn't want them to shrivel up and die. I might be vengeful, but I'm not cruel.

So Mark's still down there. Bob starts rocking back and forth. Get me out I need to tell his family.

I said I turned him into a clam. I didn't say he was down there. He types something into his computer. He shows us a video of a banquet hall filled with people in a food line. I had the annual benefit for the homeless. My daddy's many charities I now run. We had Clam chowder that night. He laughs. We had a blast.

You ate him.

No, the homeless people did. Apparently, the meat isn't very good.

You bastard.

Why are you telling us this?

Don't be stupid kid. He's going to kill us.

Just you. He reaches for a button on the intercom, take Mr. Ford and feed him to the clams. The staff comes in and grabs him. He starts to scream, but no use. They drag him out and then there is only the two of us. I don't say anything. Hoping he forgot about me. Don't worry Harold, I didn't forget about you.

So what are we going to do now?

You seem to like it here. I nod. Good. We like you here.

I smile. Thank you.

How would you like to be on my staff.

I'd like that. I know how much you love these clams. I see a real passion in you.

Yes, I truly do.

I want to give you the access you desire.

I see the sun shine from underwater. The blue sky coloring the waves. What a view. Robert offered me a chance to study the

Bivalvia without restriction and I don't regret it. I have access to the colony 24 hours a day. My new position was hard to handle at first. But after a few months I left like I've always been here. Cemented to my new community. Built on top of each other. Working together. To feed and clean the lake. To survive and multiply. Sometimes I miss my old life. I think of Janice. I hope she's happy. Maybe she was able to find a more fitting husband. I even see my grad students diving and researching our colony. I wave, but they never wave back. However, I don't mind. I'm sure they'll have great careers. I think about my mistakes, but everything washes away in time. The push and pull of the tide tells me it's that time of the season. I open my shell and watch the cloud of seamen flow in the current like seeds in the wind.

Brick Phone

He is strapped tightly to a table. A drug injected into his body to incapacitate him. A man in a dirty doctor's coat holding a vile of clear liquid and an eye dropper whispers to him. This is going to hurt.

One drop of the clear liquid into his eye he feels burning starting at his head and spreads down to his toes. A sensation of his soul being ripped from his body. The next thing he knew he was across the room witnessing his body in a vegetative state. Out of body and helpless to what the man is doing. It is what he imagines hell is like.

He screams. Waking up on a sheetless mattress in a windowless room. The room walls are cinder blocks and a dirt floor. A dim light dangles from the middle of the room illuminating a toilet without a lid. A phone randomly laying in the dirt. He runs over hoping it is his. It has been stripped of any signifier it is. His blue case, the crack in the screen going from left to right, top to bottom. This phone looks like a newer model. He presses down on the start button. The phone shakes in disagreement. Wrong password. No reception anyway. Great. He throws the phone. He hears a low buzz coming from the direction of the phone he just threw. He walks over and picks it up.

He almost throws it again, but there is a text message on the dusty screen. You're in danger.

He is at first scared, then thinks no shit. He texts back I know. A text bubble followed by a text; he doesn't know some of the phones work.

Where are you? He texts. Whoever is texting him can't be in the same situation he is.

In the next room.

Who are you?

My name is Jessie. What's your name?

He texts, Brad. He tries to delete it. He shouldn't have given his real name. The phone won't delete the message.

Nice to meet you. I think we've been abducted.

I think so too. Then he texts, are you Jessica Franklin?

How'd you know?

Your face is all over the news.

He remembers seeing articles and getting amber alerts of a missing college girl. She is a cute blonde freshman. She recently went missing. The news and the police fear she might have been a victim of the Splitter, the latest serial killer in these parts. A few months ago, the police and homeless people alike started to find mutilated bodies dumped in rivers and along highways. They say the Splitter's M.O. isn't like anything they've seen before. The bodies are all ages, genders, races. The victims' skin is split like a hot dog that's been cooking for too long and their bones are rubber. When they emptied their stomachs, they found every victim was fed well. Leafy greens and fine meats. If they hadn't been so destroyed the bodies would have belonged to extremely heathy people. However, all the news about the Splitter vanished about a week or so ago. There wasn't anything on the news outlets or social media. All the articles and posts had been deleted.

But he feels like he shouldn't believe her. It's too odd. He decides to test her. How long have you been here?

It's hard to tell with no windows, but maybe three weeks. That checks. Victims disappear and their bodies are found a few weeks later.

You don't have any windows either?

No, I'm sleeping on a dirty mattress with a dirt floor. Strange, how many rooms can the Splitter have. But he'd seen the pictures of mangled bodies and thinks anyone with that kind of time can build a labyrinth of terror.

He still doesn't believe it's her. I don't mean to be rude, but how do I know this isn't the person who kidnapped me?

A text bubble and then a picture of Jessie. Not the cheerleader the news posts, but a haggard young woman almost unrecognizable. There is a long pause as Brad goes back and forth on whether to trust her, but now it seems more likely she is who she says she is. Forgetting about the test. He decides to believe it's her.

Jessie, I have something to tell you. He doesn't wait for her to text back. We've been kidnapped by the Splitter.

What's that?

He's a serial killer.

He's been experimenting on me. It's killing me.

How? He texts back because he's seen the bodies.

The texts start rolling in. He makes me eat food. I pass out. Wake up strapped to this table. My body burns like I'm being split open. He thought of that dream he woke up screaming from.

We need to get out of here. He interrupts the rolling texts. That happened to me too. He texts franticly. I thought it was a dream. That's how they always seem. Then right after. How can we escape?

I don't know how big is he.

Big.

Maybe I can fight him.

You can't. He thought this is a strange comment.

You've never seen me.

If you're hear. He was able to get you. She has a good point. But ouch.

Can you slip by? Like doesn't he bring food. The Splitter has to

open the door. That's when he's venerable.
I'm too weak.
You don't have much time. He explains. Usually, victims disappear and their bodies are dumped three to four weeks later.
Is that going to happen to me?
No. He texts, then continues, we're getting out of here.
Ok.
We have to resist.
I think the food reacts with whatever is in the eye drops. It's supposed to make it less painful. Whatever's in those drops turns you into a conductor. He lingers a moment on this because he had no idea what it meant. He messages a question mark. Jessica is a college student. He didn't remember majoring in quantum physics. How do you know that? There is a long pause. He waits a few more minutes, but there is nothing. Is she dead? He texts Jessie. The metal door scraps open. A man over six feet tall in a doctor's coat walks in. He is carrying a plate of food. It smells so good. He is starving. The phone buzzes, but he can't look down. He puts the phone behind him. The man isn't wearing mask or anything to hide his identity. He is lanky with black balding hair. Thick black rimmed glasses that disappear into what's left of his hair. He places the tray at the foot om the bed.
The phone buzzes again. Did you hear that? He doesn't answer and the man goes on to speak. Hello, my name is…
Please let me go.
But I'm going to be set free.
I won't say anything. Please let me go.
I can't the experiment already started.
Where is Jessie?
Who?
The girl.
We've had lots of girls.
The girl on the news.
I don't watch the news. He pauses. Now I'm going to need you to eat and drink everything on…
I'm not doing shit.

Not this again.

I know who you are. You're the Splitter.

Who told you that? He screams. That's slander. The man puffs his cheeks and slowly lets the air out.

I thought you said you didn't watch the news.

He grinds his teeth. Fine. Don't eat. Suit yourself. The experiment will continue.

I'm no guinea pig. He kicks the tray of food. Splattering every-where.

The man looks at the stains on the wall. Takes another breath.

I'm not cleaning that up. Do you understand the opportunity you're wasting?

You kidnapped me.

Do you know how hard it is to find volunteers? He throws his hands up. It's fine. You'll just be another reject. He backs up out of the doorway. Their gaze never breaks and he slams the door. Alone again, he tries to pull together what just happened. What did the Splitter mean by opportunity or reject? Then he remem-bers his plan to get free. He takes out the phone. Looks down at the text.

It reads, he told me. Something about an experiment. He wants to type back, but couldn't rise his arms. He slumps on the bed passed out.

Brad wakes up strapped to a table again. Staring up at a ceiling. He tries to go back asleep, but the man comes into his eye line. Hello, the man says not smiling. He tries to spit in the man's face, but it failed. The spit just runs down his face. If you had eaten and drank everything as like I told you, you might have hit me in my face. The food acts like a lubricant. Anyway, since you kept interrupting me, I'm going to say my spiel now.

He wants to scream, but he can't. Must be it's the drugs. He could feel the burning growing as the seconds tick away.

The man continues, my name is Joesph Celine and we're going to conduct an experiment on you to upload your consciousness in the Celine-O-Verse. We're still working on the name. To put it simply we can transport your electrical energy, which is your consciousness into the computer or any device that can connect to the internet. Crazy you say. Maybe, my family and friends thought so and abandoned me. Especially when I said let's start human trails. However, the trust fund is all I need. People have been slandering my name on the internet, calling me the Splitter and serial killer, once I prove these experiments work, I find out who they are I'll sue them. So if you pay attention and listen to what I say you might be the first successful person to be uploaded in the Celine-O-Verse. Instead of being rejected and having to figure out what to do with the incomplete information. Nothing to say. Let's get started then.

He tries to protest, but the burning is becoming too much and its waves wash over him. Joesph flips a switch he starts to feel an even worse intense burning all over is body. However, this time his consciousness is ripped from his body and catapulted into a blinding white light. He feels himself fall into a membrane, which the weight of his body breaks through easily.

He finds himself in a train station instead of being strapped to a table. White titled with double stairs going to the surface. He turns and sees a train. He starts to yell for the train to stop, but before he can say anything he is vaulted back to the table again. He passes out and after an unspecific amount of time he wakes up. Still on the table. His body is smoking. His eyes still blurry settle on a shape that focuses into Joesph. Looking defeated.

You're really going to have to listen to me. The reaction between the food and the chemicals makes the transition between the two worlds easier. Like lubricant.

Fuck you.

I'm giving you an opportunity to make history and this is how you repay me.

You kidnapped me.

What were you doing with your life. His face twists trying to hold back tears. Other than rolling around in shit with the rest of the pigs. His voice echoes in the small room. Ok, fine. I kidnapped you and the others. But I want to give you something that you won't understand unless I forced you to see it.

Why won't you just let me go?

Like I told you. The experiment has already started. That means your body is dying and now I must transfer your consciousness, so you don't get stuck.

Stuck. You mean die.

Great now you're paying attention. We're on a time schedule, I'd love to leave you in a parking lot. But you'd burst into flames within a few days. Your consciousness is already separated, but not free. Hence the burning. Your body is dying. Once you're uploaded you won't need a body.

But why can't you leave people alone?

You're taking too much space. With this uploading we'll be able to fill terabytes and terabytes of information. Use all that office space.

That's pathetic.

You're pathetic. Joseph yells. Brad becomes frightened, but Joesph sees it and slowly becomes calm again. Which makes him think maybe Joesph isn't being malicious. After all he'd seems to be telling the truth. He clears his throat, I'll take you back to your room.

Joesph rolls him out of the cramped laboratory and into a cooler musty hallway right into his room. Not a labyrinth of torture chambers, but only a lab and one room. Where's Jessie's room? He thinks. Joesph props the door open with the table. Joesph easily picks him up and places him on the bed. He leaves without saying a word only the soft scraping of the door closing.

He sees a light and hears a low buzz. But he can't move. He only falls into sleep. He comes to with a mild headache, other than that he is fine. He smells food and kicks the tray at the end of the bed. He has thoughts about hurting Joesph's feelings, but then remembers he kidnapped him. He guesses the Stockholm syndrome must have set in. But he was talking about bursting into flames. What about that station he went to. He remembers the phone.

He can't sit up He flops up into a sitting position. He tries to put an arm out for support, but it bends, almost folds back. He screams. There is no pain. Maybe his nerves have been burned out from the experiments. Remembering the Splitters victims all had soft bones.

He wants to get to the phone to talk with Jessie. To check in. So he decides to crawl like a creature from the primordial ooze. Flapping dragging himself across the unpaved floor. He tries to grip the dirt floor, but the tips of his fingers deflate like oversized gloves. He keeps grabbing at the ground until there's enough friction to propel him forward.

He makes it to the phone and reads the text. Are you ok?

He pauses and remembers how small this torture house is. He wants to ask if she'd ever seen outside her room or maybe they're not even in the same house. Instead, he starts to types my bones are soft. However, it's not as easy. His soft fingers have no precession. They hit multiple letters on the keyboard. The phone keeps slipping out of his hand. The mass of it makes his hand bend until it falls on to the floor. He puts it on the ground. This helps. He can be more careful with his typing. Eventually, he texts back bones soft.

She immediately texts back. That happened to me.

He's barely hanging on, he blurts out, how is she still alive? And a text comes back.

I don't know. He is dumbfounded. The pause elongates as he realizes he didn't text that. She heard him say it.

He doesn't want to answer, but as the pause continues, he texts what are you doing? Then he adds, to survive.

I eat everything. Then I eat a hand full of dirt. Her texts continue, It doesn't taste good, but it seems to counteract the side effects. Prolonging the experiments. My bones are becoming harder.

He doesn't text back. That text gives him a plan. He is starving, so he'll eat everything and wash it down with a fist full of dirt. Hopefully, this will give him time. He forgets his hands have no shape. Unable to use a fork or knife he starts to shovel the clumps of food into his mouth. It is delicious. The best steak and eggs he's ever had. Washing it all down with the finest coffee.

He needs two hands to pick it up. Exhausting, but the payoff is worth it. His kidnapper should've have gone to culinary school instead. While getting stuffed he wonders how the dirt counteracts the chemicals, but the thought doesn't evolve outside of that. He eats it all and can feel the chemicals putting him to sleep. He grabs at the dirt floor and shovels clumps into his mouth.
The taste ruins the food he just enjoyed. The strange metallic taste with nothing to wash it down with. Pebbles suck between his teeth. He passes out. When he wakes, he's strapped to the table again. Joesph is there and says, this is the last time. You'll either be in the Celine-O-Verse or rejected. He prepares himself as Joesph flips the switch.
He is hurtled back into the white light and once it clears, he is in the train station again. He hears the train coming. Then he feels a burning. That's the last thing he remembers before he comes back to Joesph shaking his head.
You ate dirt. He sighs. Idiot. You're the second person to do that. He tries to speak, but can't. Everything is so painful. The still air even causes pain.
You can't talk. You burned your vocal cords and your skin split open. Your bodies will expire in a few hours. He looks away. I'll wheel you back to your room.
In his room he watches the world dim. He next feels like he's floating. He hears voices.
Yeah, too bad he cut the internet.
Those articles you wrote were pretty bad.
Nothing he didn't deserve.
Hello, he says interrupting them.
The new guys awake.
Where am I? He asked.
You're with us.
We got you so good.
What?
Fist full of dirt. God, how stupid.
We tricked you.
The phone.

The one I was talking to Jessie with.
He hears a roar of laughter.
He believed he was talking to a girl.
Bro, we made her up. It was a collective effort to fuck you over.
Fuck me over. Why?
To ruin Joesph's name.
He fucked us over. We couldn't get into the Celine-O-Verse.
So we decided that no one would get in.
Old Joe hasn't figured that out yet.
Some genius. Another roar of laughter.
We're all in the phone?
Yup.
He puts people here if they can't get to the Celine-O-Verse.
Rejects.
It destroys your body.
He says he'll figure out how to get us there, but no one believes
him.
The chatter goes on and pretty soon he can see, but not with
eyes. He sees a ceiling. The ceiling he died in. Or he transcended
in. Wherever this is, it's not death or the Celine-O-Verse. Trapped
in a phone. Rejected. Then a face, a woman in her thirties is look-
ing right at him. She looks scared. Her brown curly hair is a mess.
We got another one.
Fresh meat. Fresh meat. Fresh meat.
Who wants to trick her?
How about the new guy?
He thinks about getting ahead of them. To tell her the truth, so at
least someone could make it. But after a minute he decides, fuck
her.

Bad Marketing Campaign

She slides the small baggy across the barroom table past the puddles of melted ice and empty glasses of beer right in front of me and John. I examine its contents, two small square blue capsules.

What are these?

Hallucinogens. She says. You said you wanted hallucinogens.

Like LSD or shrooms. John says.

Oh, well this is better.

But what is it? I insist.

It's like a new one.

A new one?

Yeah, they haven't thought of a name yet.

Who's they?

My guy. She points vaguely behind her. When you asked if I could get stuff. That's who I went to.

And this is what he gave you.

Yeah.

John looks at me waiting for me to chime in, but all I say is how much?

You really want to get fucked up.

We're celebrating. Which is true. We worked hard on our panel called Out with the New about how to automate the already automated retail market.

She shrugs. Twenty bucks.

Do you take venmo?

Cash only.

I reach for my wallet and pull out two grimly ten dollar bills. I politely straighten them and hand the bills to her. She folds them and puts the bills into her pocket. Thanks. She smiles. What are you guys celebrating?

Nothing important. I pretend to look at the pill she gave me, wanting to back to my hotel room.

Nothing important. John says. We did a hell of a great panel. Automating the retail market.

You're here for the convention too. What are you guys banker?

Sale, John says continuing this conversation.

Who for?

Perry and Perry.

Never hear of them.

What do you do other then sell drugs? I ask. Or is this your full time gig? I interrupt rather rudely.

Ads.

Really, John says curiously.

Yeah, with Celine Advertising. She looks at me. And this isn't a drug deal. It's networking. She slides her card across to me and John. Maude Gowan in black Helvetica type set looking up from the table.

John snatches it aggressively. He examines the card. I've heard of you. His eyes light up remembering. Oh, you were on that panel. The future of Ads. Yup, that was me.

Tired and wanting to get fucked up more, I excuse myself from the conversation. Walking out into the cool night, the streets are crowd with business men and women from the Conference this weekend. Hurrying in and out of bars and alleys. I look at the

blue square in the translucent baggy between my two fingers.
I smile. Well, fuck it, I say to the crowds of people. Walk back
through the cold to my hotel room.
Walking through the empty hall and up the elevator to my room
I start regret my decision. I look at the small baggy again. I could
do it later. It'll still earlier. Go to another bar and have another
drink. Forget the whole thing. But I know that won't happen. I'll
go to a bar. Not talk to anyone and leave once I finish my one
beer. I shrug and put the capsule in my mouth and swallow it. I
goes down hard and I nearly cough it up.
Just as I get a hold of my disposition, the coughing gets worse.
The force of the heaving makes me think my lungs are going to
pop out of my mouth. I swallow and look up at the large hotel
mirror. It's convex and I watch black lines emanate from the
center. I get up to examine them. Web like tendrils. I follow one
strand unfurling down the mirror and touch it. It spreads even
more. I flinch away and I see it growing on my fingers. It seeps
into my skin and I feel every nerve ending heat and burn up. I
scream. That's when I hear someone else in the room.
I hear shuffling from behind. Turning my head, I see a brownish
figure. Tubular. It doesn't move like a person, more like a worm.
Twitching. I turn back to the mirror and see a creature clearer. No
eyes only coils of fungal patched skin with rows of spikes. Poking
and sniffing the air.
Turning what might be its head at me it speaks, shshshtigfrail-
lashun. I scream again and run out the door and down the
hallway. I see the elevator, but the tendrils from the mirror keep
pace. I run down the stairs. It continues to follow me. Whatever
crawled into my skin is working like an anchor, making me run
harder. I feel it burning through my skin. I make it outside. The
cold air hits me. The city is moving, but not with festival fun.
The street is covered in the patches of skin and spikes. It bulges
as if there is a large worm like thing underneath. The streetlights
bend and slithering towards me. The buildings gyrate and hiss,
shshrigrailshut. Bellowing in my bones
I fall to the moving ground. Curl up in a ball. Sweating in the

fridged air without a coat. The screeching and hiss in my ear. I start crying. Then it stops. I slow unfurl myself. It was all a hallucination.

Fuck, I say to the normal city streets. It felt, so real. I stand up, dust myself off. I turn right into one of those spikes from that creature. I feel it grind against my skin like grating cheese. I touch where the pain is and my hand is speckled in red blood. I almost faint, but that thing is twisting. I run again. My legs burn with exhaustion, but I'm so horrified. I watch the hallucination start again bending around me. I keep running until I see a strange light. Bright and stale shinning from a building. The fungal tendrils don't grow there. It's a strip mall. No, it's a furniture store. Celine Furniture. I run, hopefully whatever this is will stop. Through the empty parking lot and run towards the double doors. There's no way it's open, but the doors gently open.

I feel the spikey fungus drain out of the cut in my hand in the bright warm light of the store. Why can't they come in here? I don't care. I walk further into the furniture store. Surprised it's still open. Glassing the store there isn't anyone in it. I continue to walk further, pretending to peruse. It's odd because I feel perfectly normal like the trip is over.

Can I help you? A woman's voice from behind me. I turn and there's an old woman. Short, spectacle, and greying.

I'm just looking at your wonderful selection.

Are you alright? Looking me up and down. I think you cut your hand.

I look down at wound. Still bleeding. I put it behind my back. Yeah. I'm fine.

Do you want a band aid?

No, I hesitate. I'll be alright.

Well, maybe while you look around, I can make you some tea.

Sure. Not wanting to be rude.

Have a seat.

I sit at the nearest white loveseat. As soon as I sit, I fall sleep.

I open my eyes and everything looks the same, but it's day. My hand is bandaged. I get up and nearly knock a cup of tea off the display table. I look around. Still no one here.

I run back to my hotel room. I argue with the front desk to give me another key card. After they give it to me. I unlocked the door and find the room demolished. I don't remember doing any of this. I don't have time for it though as I have to check out in a half an hour. I take a shower and pack my things. The last thing I do before I leave is call John.

Hey.

Hey, what happened? I've been trying to reach you.

I took that pill.

How'd that go?

It was the most insane night I ever had.

Great. Can't wait to try it.

You didn't take yours.

No, I was more interested in Maude.

Who?

The woman who gave us the drugs.

Is she still there?

No, she left an hour ago. He pauses. Hey, do you want to get some breakfast?

I got to check out.

Me too. There a place right here that's open.

Fine.

I hang up the phone and try to clean up. I flip over the bed, but find the mattress has been cut into. Then the nightstand is underneath it smashed. It keeps getting worse. I just need to leave. Then I catch a glimpse in the mirror. One of those fungus things. Trignail. It hisses.

I run out of the room before it can scratch me again. How much long is this hallucination going to last. If it is a hallucination. I slow down to think about that. Didn't Maude say it was new. So it wouldn't work like LSD or shroom. Those fungus must be a residual effect, like an acid flashback. But they're so real. I breath deep, it's gone. I go check out.

Watching John scoop eggs and bacon into his mouth is more disgusting than usual. Maybe it's from the lack of good sleep or another effects of that pill. The white plastic skin of the eggs. The smell of them opening, draining the thick yellow yolk. John's chewing and sipping coffee.

Not hungry?

Not really. Hey, do have Marg's number?

Who?

Marg. I pause. The girl you slept with. Who gave us the drugs.

Maude.

Maude.

No. He says and goes back to eating.

Do you still have her card?

Nope. Shoveling more food into his face. I probably left it at the bar.

I look past John and see the fungus tendrils starting to grow up the booth's dividers up the restaurant's walls. The terror starts to rise, but I try to control it. I don't want to freak out in front of everyone. Are you almost done?

Yeah, why you want to go back so soon? We've still got a whole day of seeing this city before going home.

Oh no, I wanted to go see someone before we left anyway. Should be fine.

I look back up and the fungus is gone. I sigh in relief. Soon the check comes and we pay and leave. We get into John's truck and pull out of the parking lot. I asked John to look up Celine Furniture on the GPS. It is a few blocks away, so we drive there.

You need some new furniture?

No, Maude worked for Celine Ads and this is Celine Furniture.

You're really obsess with Maude.

She gave me a drug that I'm still seeing crazy shit.

You're still tripping?

I don't know.

Sounds like fun.

I don't say anything. I wanted to see that old lady I met last night. To apologize and to see if she knows anything about all of this. I just open the door and walk towards the furniture store. All around the parking lot and on the billboards visible are pastured yellow signs saying Big Sale in big black letters. Weird, I think, it seems almost closed when I was in it last. I sense John is behind me. My pace quickens. We walk in and all the lights are on, but there is no one here.

Nice selection, John says.

Where is she? I go deeper into the store looking for that old woman I met with the tea.

She? He follows.

Darting here and there, around the table and chairs, finally finding her in a tiny office in back. Hi.

She jumps and after a second recognizes me. Oh hi. She laughs. You scared me.

Sorry.

You're the first repeat consumer I've had in a while. She pauses. Or did you come back for some more tea.

Oh no thank you. I embarrassed. I just saw your store is called Celine Furniture and I was wondering if it's any relation to Celine Ads?

She shrugs. No. This store, my family owns it. I don't know of an advertising firm.

Oh, so they didn't create those signs outside.

The Big Sale signs. She smiles. No, those are unfortunately our competitor's signs. They're going to put us out of business. They're just across the alley.

Oh, sorry to hear that. Surprised at my honest concern.

She waves away my concern. Don't worry. It's probably for the best. Leaking money for years.

Well, I'm sorry I couldn't be of more help.

Oh no.

John comes up carrying a table chair. How much for the set?

She glances. You can have it for $100.

Sold. He hands her a credit card. Lifting the chair over his head and disappearing again.

Rolling my eyes as I help John carry four chairs to his truck. The woman comes up to the truck as we climb in it. She's carrying two cups of teas. The tags blowing in the wind. She wishes us

luck on finding that woman. I grab the two drinks and thank her.
I hand one to John. She walks back in and we speed out of the
parking lot. John rolls down his window and throughs the cups
of tea into the nearest dumpster. I am offended he did that. A
feeling of protectiveness towards that old lady.
What?
I didn't say anything.
I hate tea.
Fine.
What do you like that lady?
I didn't say anything. There is an awkward silence. What do you
want to do now?
Let's get fucked up.
Sure.
We go to a bar John wanted to check out. It seems plain from
the brick exterior, but on the inside the music is loud and people
stand screaming at each other in small groups holding beer. It's
fine with me. I want to forget what this town has done to me.
Maude. The fungus. Although I want to come back to the fur-
niture store. John finds a high top to sit at and I order the first
round. Bringing the beers back to the table we cheers and down
the pints. After the second, we decide to get a pitch of beer.
As I start pouring the pitcher into my glass, I find I can't feel the
tip of my index finger. I look down at it. It looks swollen. Then a
black dot forms like a black head and becomes a violent diagonal
black line. I hide my finger from view. Hopefully, no one saw it.
I rush to the bathroom. I go to one of the doorless stalls. It has
become a crooked webs spiraling down my finger. Any drunken-
ness I built up is gone now. I have to leave now. Hiding my hand,
I rush out of the bathroom back to our table.
Hey, do you want to leave?
No, John looks around at the people. Why? Everything alright?
I kind of want to go home.
He shrugs. I'm too fucked up to drive.
I can drive.
He looks at me. Shrugs. Hands me the keys. I help him out of

the bar and up into the truck. Walking around the front, I feel the spines from the fungus grow up my hand and into my wrist and forearm.

Pulling out of the bar parking lot and trying to get to the highway. One eye on the road the other watching the black lines spread across my body. The headlights beam on the road which is moving up and down in a black spiraling web. SShTrigstale. I jump as I hear it ring inside my head. I scream and look at John, who is passed out. I take my eye off the road and when I look up again and smash into a streetlight. The air bags deploy.

I wake to on the side of the road to smelling salts. I watch John get taken away in an ambulance. The fungus growing on my arm is gone, their voices still ring in my ear. Stalebrigssha. Someone snaps his fingers in front of my face.

Hey.

I don't say anything.

Are you alright? What happened?

Something, I think of what just happened, jumped out at us.

Have you been drinking?

I'm the designated driver.

Alright, just sit there. I'll be right back. He walks off.

In my state I still hear the fungus' voice. Soft, but still there.

I look around and I'm on an offramp looking down at Celine Furniture. The sign burns my eyes in the night. I get up and start walking towards it. Stumbling over the pedestrian bridge, down a backstreet and after wandering in the wet dark I somehow find my way to the empty parking lot of the Celine Furniture parking lot.

Walking into the warm breath of the furniture store. The voice screech and go silent. All of my worries go away. I wonder around until I find the old woman.

Hi. I say.

Hello, you look like you took a tumble.

You could say that.

How can I help you?

I took this drug. She stiffens. But I don't think it was a drug.

What happened when you took it?

I've been going crazy? I don't understand what I've been seeing. I don't understand why I'm spilling the beans to her. I just came out of me.

Instead of being repulse she asks, Crazy how?

I've been seeing these creatures. Like giant fungal worms with these spikes and tendrils everywhere.

She silently nods.

And they scream at me.

Is that it?

About the long and the short of it.

She walks over to a small book case in her office and looks through the old moldy books. She picks a particularly old book. She flips to a page and shows me. Do they look like this? The image in the book is an exact replica of the creatures I've been seeing.

My God, yes. I take the book dumbfounded. It's designed with strange drawings and stretches. Maybe it's a language. Did she know all along? What are they?

I can't pronounce their name, but they are summoned by a person who needs help.

Help. Do they not want me to do drugs?

You probably weren't the one who summoned them.

Maude? Does she want to kill me? Are these things trying to kill me? Because one of them scratched me.

She takes the book back. It says they are trying to tell you something. Probably marking you.

Marking me for what?

They chose you to help.

Help with what?

What do they scream at you?

Nonsense. Trignail. Trying to remember more. Stallebrig. I stop. Stalle Brig. Big Sale. After combining and linking it in my head. It's big sale. I yelp. It's those signs. That store.

That's quite a consequence.

What should we do? She shrugs. Are these people evil or some-

thing?
You probably know my opinion, but what do you think?
I've never met them.
They're just across the street.
You think I should go over and see?
Couldn't hurt. These things might stop chasing you.
I could go and take look around. Then come back.
Sounds like a plan. I go to get up, but she takes my hand. Hold on. She bends down, reaching into a nook and when she gets up says, just in case those things want help from a malevolent furniture store. She puts a gun in my hand. I hesitate. This has been a weird afternoon, but then I think of what I've seen within the last 48 hours, I might need it.
Thank you.
Good luck.
I open the door and can see the store across the alley. The competitor, already throbbing malevolently in the barking dawn.
The fungi are screaming big sale over and over again. There are already people coming in and out of the store. They seem infected with something even worse than those tendrils. It's like a rot. Their skin is peeling off revealing a black and green exoskeleton. What is this place doing to its customers. I cock the gun I'm holding in my jeans pocket.
I enter the automatic doors and see the horror. The furniture are devices of torture tearing customers screaming limb from limb. Only to be reassembled in ghastly ways. The staff watching the new creations limp away to their hysteric laughter. Unafraid, I walk up to one of the demonic staff.
They smile with their sharp teeth. Can I help you, sir? With a woman's voice. Without saying anything, I press the gun up to its face and pull the trigger. There's a scream and I watch everything scatter. I don't stop shooting at the demons until the gun clicks. That's when reality rushes back and the screaming in my head cuts out immediately. I guess my job is done. The demons and torture devices are replaced by white tiles and corpses with pooling blood.

Suddenly, someone grabs me and pin me to the ground. I'm put in handcuffs. It's the police. They push my face into the cool tile floor. They force me up. I'm pushed out the automatic doors again where flashing blue and red lights greet me. Squad cars are dashed everywhere. A crowd has gathered. We push through the docile crowd and the old woman is one person I recognize. She puts her hand on my chest and mouths thank you to me. I watch her disappear into the crowd. After that the police duck my head into the police car and we speed away.

Consumer

Driving back to the police station around midnight. Six hours left to go. Instead of taking the winding backroads, I decided to take the highway to hurry up and wait for my shift to be over. There are no other cars, so it should be quick. While driving down the highway 95, two exits away, the lights begin to flicker. Highway Patrol's going to have some explaining to do tomorrow. Then the lights black out. My headlights the only thing shining. I start to panic and pick up the radio. Suddenly, the lights go back on. I find myself heading right for a guard rail. I cock the wheel and right the car to go straight.

My eyes focus on a white figure a little way down the road. When I get closer, I see a man in a cape running in the breakdown lane. I flash my siren, but he ignores it. I speed up to him and see it's not a cape, but a coat. A lab coat. A doctor. Sure, but by the look of him he might have found those clothes in a dumpster. They're black streaked, worn and full of holes. The bottom of his white shoes detached, flopping as his feet hit the blacktop. He must

have been running for a while because he is hobbling and glowing
pink in my headlight's beams.
I drive about a hundred feet in front of him and parking. I start
walking towards him with my hands up. When he gets closer, I
say. Hey Buddy, what are you running from?
Run. No one's safe. Just got to run. Horsely screaming so close
to my face I can feel his hot moist breath. He zigzags around me
and the police car. He just keeps running.
This aggravates me, so I turn. Stop running, I command and
chase him. I sprint towards him quickly as I am starting fresh. I
tackle him.
He squirms and I squeeze him even more. No, you don't understand. We've got to leave.
Pinning him to the ground, I take out zip ties, Yeah, yeah, yeah. I
pull the chord and tighten them around his wrists.
I lift him up. He still tries to get away. He is taller than me but I'm
much stronger, so I whip him around to go where I want him to
go. I put him in the back of the car and call the station.
Station.
Go ahead Roy.
I've got a homeless man in my car. Maybe on drugs or crazy. I'm
coming to the station, so get ready.
Oh boy. Sounds like a dozy.
I let go of the receiver, you're not kidding, I say to myself. I look
in back and see the homeless man is passed out, snoring. A lan-
yard badge pinned to his lapel. I reach for it. His picture frowning
back at me. Michael T. Picard. Turns out he's a scientist. Celine
Labs. The address 243 Service Road Celineton. That's 45 minutes
away from here. He ran that far.
Station.
Yes, Roy.
Could you also look up Celine labs?
Sure thing.
Thanks.
I begin driving my way to the station again. The drive is calm
until we hit the last red light before my destination. Pulling up to

it with my blinker on, I notice the traffic light is out. I scan the town and there are no lights at all. I drive cautiously. I see the station even from a few hundred feet away. It's the only building with any lights on. A beacon. Thank God for backup generators. I turn into the parking lot and cut the ignition. The snoring stops and he pops up in the back seat.

Where are we?

We're at the police station. You'll be safe.

He presses his face right up against the plexiglass divider. You don't understand man. There is no more safe. There's only running.

Listen, whatever drugs you're on are going to wear off and you're really going to regret taking them.

I'm not on drugs. Don't you understand. They're coming.

Well, when they get here let me know. Until then just calm down would you.

I get out and open the back seat. He flails around, but after a second, I grab a leg and pull him out of the car. I hold him with one arm, so he doesn't run off. He resists and is yelling about these people who are coming. How we need to run. Finally, after a few committed minutes I manage to get him through the doors.

Sally, I say to an empty receptionist desk.

Her head pops up. What?

The whole town's lost electricity has the mayor called?

No, she says. Who's he? Referring to the man.

Michael. The homeless man I called about. He won't stop squirming. I want to put him an integration room. Is one available?

Everything available.

Good. Get the rookie and have this man questioned. She gets on the radio. I throw the lanky man onto one of the lobby chairs.

Stay there. I point at him.

He'll be down in a minute.

Try getting a hold of the mayor. We might have to follow a protocol. I take a deep breath as I can already see the rookie fumbling down the brightly lit highway. Probably sleeping in the storage room again.

Like an emergency?

Something like that. The rookie fixes himself. Before he can say anything I cut in, get this man into an interrogation room.

What'd he do?

He's either on drugs or running from something else.

Sure, the rookie says, come on sir.

Michael refuses.

I lift him up and hand him to the rookie. You might have to use a little force.

He gives me an uncomfortable glance, but nods and takes him away.

Hey Sally.

Hey yourself.

Did you get any information about that Celine Labs?

Of course. She slides a folder over. There's a small police station there, but I couldn't get a hold of them.

Are there any security feeds from the town?

She shakes her head. None that are working.

Small towns. I shake my head. Always ten years behind. Anyway, keep trying. Let me know if anything changes.

Alright, she frowns.

If you need me, I'll be at my desk.

She gives me the ok symbols and I walk off to my desk in the back. There are four desks mine, the rookies, and two empty desks. No one has filled them yet. The chief is the only one with an office, but he's on vacation.

I pour myself a cup of coffee and crack open the folder Sally gave me. Reading the articles that were printed off I can't find anything that unusual. It's a privately funded lab. Looking through miscellaneous documents everything seems above board. The town is only five thousand people. Remembering what Michael said, they're coming. But who? From what I can tell the population is mostly people under 18 and above 45. Maybe he was making a new drug and took it himself. I've heard of that happening. Mad scientist breaking the rules.

Roy.
I jump, what's up rookie.
Can you talk to this guy?
Why?
He's saying crazy things and no one can get a hold of the police
station or mayor or anything in that town.
I guess can come and show you how real police do it. I laugh.
He does not laugh. I'm serious.
Alright, I'll be there in a minute.
Walking into the interrogation room, Michael is no less relaxed.
His eyes are almost plates. The rookie says, tell him what you told
me.
There's no time. We need to get out of here. We need to evacuate
the town. Maybe the state or country.
What the hell did you people do? I say. Nuclear fallout. Some
chemical spill.
Just listen. The rookie says trying to calm everything down. Tell
him, he goads him.
Fine. Michael clears his throat. We need to leave because the con-
sumers are coming.
Like shoppers? I ask.
No, their people that consume everything.
I'm not following.
They put stuff in the water. The rookie says.
I still don't understand.
Jesus, Michael whispers loudly and starts, David.
David? David who?
David Brown. We worked together at Celine Labs.
Can we contact him? Because we can't contact anyone from
where you were running from.
He's dead. Everyone is probably dead.
I'm listening.
I'm trying to tell you.
Alright. Then spit it out.
David and I were experimenting with hormonal messaging and
AI.

What does that mean?

Roy you're going to love this, the rookie says, it's like if a company wants us to buy a certain toothpaste, the computer creates a hormone to put in the water to make us buy it.

Really. Looking at Michael.

In a sense yes. Michael sighing almost offended, that's what we were doing.

Why would you want to do that?

To sell products better, create more stable marketplaces, and make the perfect consumer.

Control people.

You could see it like that. Sure.

So, these people escaped from the lab?

Lab, we used the whole town.

What? It's the only thing I could think of to say. This man I thought was just some druggy. Now he's capable of mind control.

We put it in the town's water supply. He clarifies, the water is privately owned. And it is nontoxic.

I couldn't find words. I am so baffled.

Get this Roy, they don't even have to drink it. If they wash their dishes in it or take a shower. It seeps into their skin. He gets so excited. Tell him what you and David did. The rookie continues the conversation.

We were going to be defunded because the AI would make the hormonal commands too literal.

The rookie interrupts. Like if a company wanted to sell toothpaste the computer would make a chemical to buy the tooth paste. But all that people would buy is toothpaste. The stores were sold out and they'd eat the toothpaste and bathe in it. Crazy stuff.

Yes, thank you. Michael continues. So they were going to defund us because of that fault. David and I decides to create a hormone that would make them perfect consumers. As a joke because we thought they'd buy the town and the company.

Like Revenge.

I guess that's a better word for it. After it was made, we put it in the water.
Tell him what happened.
They started eating everything.
They became consumers that ate everything. The rookie laughs.
Have you heard of anything, so insane.
So they became cannibals.
They ate the people who didn't drink the water, but they also ate wires, asphalt, wood, plastic, grass, whatever was near them. They won't stop.
You poisoned all of those people.
Please, Michael say coldly, I made those people into death machines. It was more than they could've come up with on their own.
I get up. Can I talk to you for a second? I say to the rookie.
Sure.
We walk into out of the room and shut the door. What do you think of all this?
Do you think he's lying?
I don't know. Did he tell you anything about David?
Apparently, he's dead.
That's what we should ask next. We walk back into the room.
What happened to David Brown then?
The question made him flinch in pain. He's dead.
How?
We were watching the town be consumed. Listening to that awful clicking. I don't know why, but for some reason their jaws click. And a few of them came up to us and started eating him. I didn't help him. I just ran.
Hearing enough I stand up. Alright, put him in a holding cell.
Why?
Why. If what he is saying is true, he poisoned a town and might have been responsible for a few murders. Either way I don't want him to get free.
Didn't you hear. We have to leave. Michael pleads.
This place will protect us.

Celine Labs was better equipped.

I've heard enough. Get him out.

We're all going to die.

The rookie grabs him and starts towards the door.

Meet me in the parking lot. We're going to find out if his story has any basis in reality. The rookie nods and leaves. I run to Sally's desk. Anything?

No, everything is dead.

Shit. I try to think, but I hit a brick wall. Ok, the scientist is in the holding cell. Me and the rookie are going to drive to Celineton. Stay here. We'll hopefully be back in an hour.

Fine with me.

Before going outside, I go to the armory. The creeping idea that Michael laid out is terrifying. Whether or not it's real it gives me piece of mind to be prepared. I meet the rookie in the hallway. We collect vests and shotguns leaving the rifles and extra ammo in the station in case there really is something going on.

It's even darker outside than it was when I first arrived. A wall of darkness encroaches on the parking lot. I can't even make out outlines of buildings, streetlights, or even the road which is about twenty five yards away. There are no cars on the road only what I first think are cicadas. Strange they're out this late in the season. Then I realize the humming isn't the annoying buzzing of the insect, but a gnashing, a clicking. As if someone is unhinging their jaw. I shine a flashlight in its direction and scream.

As far as the flash light reaches there are people on all fours. Their clothes are ripped and covered in blood. Holes in their faces probably from eating everything in sight. How haven't their stomach not ruptured? Chewing clods of dirt and asphalt. Some seem to be eating bugs or small animals they found. They aren't viciously gnawing, but casually looking at whatever they've picked up and calmly bite into it. I slowly reach for my gun and point it at a bald man in a green shirt. The only object I can focus on in the pulsing mass. I hear gun shots and turn in that direction. The rookie is being overrun by five or six of them biting down on his flesh. He's screaming, but I stand frozen in a gunslinger

stance. His scream becomes higher in pitch then cut out completely when one of them tears his head from his body. I watch them eat the remains until hands grip my elbow with surprising strength. I drop my gun. I turn, but it's already too late. A fat woman with curly black hair puts my pinky and ring finger into her wet mouth and bites. Her dull teeth tear into my thin skin and soft bones. She laps up the hot blood pouring from the wound. I snatch what's left of my hand in disbelief. I only have three fingers now. I just run back to the station knowing I'm being followed. Pumping blood out of my body, not caring about the guns or the rookie or whatever's left of the town. Once through the double doors, I lock them. I'm not sure it'll help.
Stumbling to the receptionist desk. I put paper to sop up the blood. Sally, I yell. She pops her head around the corner.
What happened? She says looking at my hand.
We're being attacked.
By what?
I can't explain. Just get to the holding cells. Get Michael. We need to leave. She runs and I follow her, but she's too fast and I've lost too much blood. I give up and sit on the floor. I try to make the room stop spinning. It doesn't work. I have passed out. When I come to Michael and Sally looking down at me. Locked in one of the cells.
They're already here?
I nod.
Who's here?
I slide up the wall. These cells won't protect us.
It's too late.
Run?
Not with those things outside.
They've surrounded us.
Michael grabs me. I should you kill you.
You'll have to get in line. He throws me back to the wall.
What's going on? Sally says. Michael tries to explains, but in her disbelief, she asks a lot of questions. So many Michael screams at her. She stops talking. I hear the gnashing sound.

They've made it inside.

It's only a matter if time.

In my blood loss haze I start to hear the clicking getting louder.
I catch Michael's eyes and I know it's not good. The glass coated
wire door and windows with a heavy lock will be easy for them to
go through. Not to mention that we can hear them on the outside of the cell walls. We're trapped on all sides. They're chewing
down the heavy metal door to the holding cells and gnawing away
the walls themselves. Soon I watch as dust starts to fall on the
floor and know that they are boring through the concrete walls.
Then they break down the door. That's when the real problems
being.

The consumers crawl and bite the floor or the adjacent cells. A
few start chewing on our cell door and within no time make a
hole to enter. Michael is the closest to the hole, but before he can
move away a young man in a leather jacket grabs his shoulder and
bites down on his collar bone. Sally screams as his blood spurts
out. He tries not to be dragged away. Grabbing at whatever he
can. I try to help at first but I can make out faces in the bored
holes in the walls and think it's every man for himself. Making
a decision, I cruel up in a ball. Sally and I watch him be slowly
devoured alive. He still slams his fists and curses at me which are
quickly drowned the clicking of his creation devours him.

The noise is so loud we don't notice the screaming has stops
until we make out Michael picked apart skull. Sally and I watch
in horror at them slowly eating the rest him. He is nothing but
bones in minutes and then nothing at all within a few minutes.
The consumers don't seem to notice us yet. We think we might
be able to slip away. However, once they're done, they calmly
go back to eating the floor and the cell itself. Closing us in even
more. Biting into the plastic coat steel like it is birthday cake. The
noise is deafening.

Sally looks at me and whispers, what are we going to do?

I shrug.

What is that supposed to mean?

We're trapped.

What about a gun?

I don't have a gun.

What kind of cop are you?

Terrible one. Sighing, holding my head in what's left of my hands. Sally goes back to being a small silent ball. Putting her hands over her ears. She screams in frustration, but it's devoured by the clicking. However, it doesn't go unnoticed as a few look up and slowly stumble over to her. She kicks and punches, but they grab her attempts. Biting into Sally's foot and arm. She reaches for me, but I curl up into a tighter ball. It doesn't work because a man in a peacoat bends over me and I decide to go out fighting. His grip is so strong I can't get away. All of the punches and kicks don't affect him. He bites into me and then does it again. I scream, but he or what's left of Sally or anyone else no longer cares.